The
Otherwise
Girl

The Otherwise Girl

KEITH CLAIRE

Holt, Rinehart and Winston   *New York*

Library of Congress Cataloging in Publication Data
Claire, Keith.
  The otherwise girl.

  I. Title.
PZ4.C5850t3   [PR6053.L26]   823'.9'14   75-29789
ISBN 0-03-016681-0

FIRST EDITION

PRINTED IN THE UNITED STATES OF AMERICA

10 9 8 7 6 5 4 3 2 1

The
Otherwise
Girl

1

"Good-bye, boy," my father had said. He had become unexpectedly serious for him. "I think you may find it a bit strange down there, Matt. He'll be a bit different all on his own—in his own house, down there. Best of luck."

After that I was taken up with the journey. I had started early in the morning and now it was night. The blunt long-distance coach growled on and on beneath high and shadowed hedges, the beams of its headlights thrusting at the dark ahead, a dark over a part of the country of which I knew nothing except the stories. Here and there I could make out banks of grass and groups of trees, once a pale house—all touched with a sudden ghastly headlight color—and then the fingers of our lights rushed on elsewhere. I remember the other passengers only as pasty faces seated in their rows around me, lolling faces, sleeping faces. I can remember the driver's black-suited back. I can remember the cat's-eyes reflecting in the road, staring at us from every curve, seeming to run toward us, only to fade to darkness underneath our wheels.

Yet I stayed so awake. I was fifteen and alone and full of suppressed excitement, I suppose. I knew that after so very many hours my stop was almost here. I had two seats to myself and my bag sat on one of them and I just stared and stared through my window out at the dancing shadows, at the passing hedges. I had to press my face against the window to see at all. Once, beyond the hedges, beyond the fields, I thought I saw a blacker motionless line that must have been the hills. I knew there were hills. Then our headlights picked out a lake, a sheet of water, and, even as I took it in, our lights had turned away and I had lost lake and hills and was looking at blackness, seated all by myself in a coach and on my first trip to Elverley.

Dockhurst lived at Elverley.

You see, of all the people my father and mother knew (and there were lots of those—sometimes too many, I thought) the one I liked the best was Dockhurst. Dockhurst was the artist one. It was Dockhurst who lived in a barn down at Elverley, who sometimes visited us uninvited in London, slouching and sarcastic—amusing Mum. He would take Dad off to the pub, just when lunch was ready; he would take me round exhibition galleries—he always knew everyone behind the scenes. Outings with him were always outings to unexpected places. And Dockhurst never minded talking to me for hours, explaining things and explaining how he saw things. For everywhere we went he had to make drawings, quick little sketches, tiny paintings: of the insides of machinery in power stations, of the outsides of huge aircraft at Heathrow Airport (*he* could get permission for us to sit on a wing), of people visiting the zoo—and even from within the lion's cage (we did not have the lion with us—only the smell). I went with him when he drew the wheeling traffic from the top of Marble Arch. And even if he did live in the country he seemed to know almost everybody—the man selling long balloons down Oxford Street, the girl who sold him socks in Marks and Sparks, and, equally as well, important museum officials and the station master at Paddington. Not that Dockhurst always said so much. He would often work in public places with a notice pinned to the back of his sweater: GO AWAY—CONFOUND YOU! And to me all he might say was: "Hold this, boy." Or: "Get me some water, Matt. Where? How should I know?"

I would have to scurry round and ask strangers (which I did not much like doing) and find him his water. He would just sit on his folding stool in his grubby old slacks and his tangle of gray hair, while his nervous, clever pencil moved across his sheet of gray paper. I learned how he looked at things. Now I had to learn how he drew them. I had to draw them myself.

And so Dockhurst had invited me. . . .

ELVERLEY 2 MILES, the signboard said, vanishing away behind me in the dark.

I still remember how the road dipped down to

Elverley, how we went over a bridge and down and left and then hard left again, our brakes squealing, and then we were going under the bridge we had been over and down once more, and yet Elverley was still below us, but for the first time I could see the lights of the village.

There were rather a lot of lights, a whole yellow glow was coming up over a line of roofs and trees. I had seen drawings of Elverley—Dockhurst used to do little sketches all over his letters to me. (I should have kept all those letters—but I never did.) I knew that the coach would pull up beside the green. I knew that Dockhurst's barn was somewhere on the farther side. In a few minutes—moments—I realized, I would actually be seeing Dockhurst, Dockhurst standing feet apart and his hands pushed into his pockets, thinking of something somewhere different and yet still watching me and everyone from the corner of an eye.

The road narrowed sharply and we slowed and were in light and this was the main street. All the houses seemed ablaze with light and I realized that there were people everywhere. The whole village was awake, visited, cars parked head to tail—and then we were coming out beside the green, pulling to a stop, and there was actually a big crowd.

I stood up to see what was happening.

It was a midnight fair! There was blaring pop music, a row of stalls with flaring oil lamps, people selling, people shying coconuts, a small roundabout, tents, marquees, people in funny hats, people waving streamers. Out in the middle of the green there was a huge bonfire, yellow flames sparking and leaping against the darkness— and there were dancers. There were people in white masks and long cloaks and carrying tall torches—there must have been a dozen of them, stamping and turning in a great wide circle. The dancers were closing in toward the fire. . . .

Our driver slid a little wearily out of his seat. "Elverley," he said. "One for Elverley."

It pulled me up sharp. I suddenly realized that I really was arriving, and I grabbed my bag and had to crab my way up toward the door. Some of the other passengers were waking up, necks were being craned. Someone even took out his camera.

"They do it every year," the driver remarked, as if that explained something. "Got any other luggage, boy?"

I hadn't. The driver opened the door for me, and then I dropped out of the warm coach and onto the road. The door slid shut, I stood back, and then, with a slight toot, the coach nosed out behind the crowd. For a moment I could only see its huge taillights glaring out like angry eyes, then one winked, and the coach that had been my proper place all day had gone.

The night air was sharp, yet acrid with smoke, and my ears were smothered by the metallic beat of the amplified music—so that, of my senses, only my eyes were alive to what was happening. And then, all at once, that music was switched off—dead! For the first time I heard the crackling of that bonfire, could almost hear the heavy silence of the surrounding crowd, could really hear the shuffle of the dancers' feet. But the dancers stopped. A woman had begun to sing, and though I could not make out the words, what she sang seemed so far away and so sad that the whole of Elverley seemed to pause—everything seemed to stop, to listen. There was only this voice, the sputter of that fire and of those torches.

It was at this exact moment that I realized Dockhurst was not here. There was so much to see, it was so unexpected, that I had not looked for him before. But then nobody had taken any notice of my coach. It was as if there'd never been a coach. There was only me standing here now, standing at the back of a crowd in the dark of a strange village.

A slight sense of unwanted panic twisted a little in the pit of my stomach.

I suppose I could ask. But how many people in this crowd would know where Dockhurst's barn was, anyway? Only a few of them could be locals. I wondered what I ought to do. The coach hadn't been . . . I looked at my watch. The coach certainly hadn't been early. And the driver had *said* Elverley.

I stood staring at the flickering light on the faces of the watching crowd. I could still hear the singing. I could not see the singer.

I hoped the driver had said Elverley. I would look a complete fool getting out at the wrong village at this time of night. At least I knew that Elverley did have a green. But perhaps they all had greens round here. It was at this moment that I realized that the village church was just behind me, that I was leaning against the low stone wall around the churchyard, that I could see the gravestones and a square tower hanging in the darkness. A notice board! But of course.

I could just make it out: ELVERLEY PARISH CHURCH. That was a relief. I decided that I had better wait here just a little longer.

My eye drifted back to the dancers. I could hardly

hear the singer now, the dancers had started again; somewhere in the background someone was playing a fiddle, and the hooded dancers were turning on the spot. I remember staring, fascinated and puzzled by turns, still clutching at my bag.

"I think you must be Matt," a girl's voice said into my ear.

I nearly fell over my bag. The girl was sitting on the churchyard wall, she was almost beside me. She was just sitting up there, bare legs and bare feet dangling, short skirt and sweater. I could have sworn that she hadn't been there before. I hadn't heard her climb up there. It wasn't easy to make out her face in the shadows.

"Yes—I'm Matt. How do you know?" I managed to say.

"And you're going to stay with Dockhurst—for a week?" It was a voice that half teased as it spoke.

"That's right," I agreed. At least, I decided, it did look as if I were expected.

I felt her hand grip my shoulder, she leaned forward and then dropped lightly down onto the road. She was hitching at her skirt, tucking in her sweater. I saw her face. She wrinkled her nose when she smiled and it was a nose with freckles on it—all her face had freckles on it.

"How do I know?" she asked and she was still teasing. I saw her tongue come out between her lips —almost as if it, too, had popped out to look round. I reckoned that she was almost my age, maybe a bit younger. It's hard to tell with girls.

"Well—everybody else is watching the dancing over there. And this is where the coach stops and

7

you've got that bag with you. So you must be Matt—and you are!"

"Isn't Dockhurst coming, then?" I asked. All along I had been picturing Dockhurst's joking, half-contemptuous greeting.

"Expect he's working."

She had turned her back to the fair and the dancers, and I could hardly see her face for shadow. She was more interested in me—almost as if I were something out of a museum. She looked at what I wore, fingered my jacket, looked at my shoes, even lifted the bag to see how heavy it was. I did not know what to say.

"Sometimes," she went on, "Dockhurst doesn't know or care where he is—or even what day it is. But I like that. My mum goes to see him—though most of the village think he's mad. You know he mostly lives by himself now? But you don't have to worry—I think you're lucky—Dockhurst's a marvelous cook."

I wasn't paying too much attention to what she said. Over her shoulder I could see that the dancing on the green had quickened. I could see that there was a small dancer among them, a single unmasked dancer—though I could not make out if it was boy or girl. It seemed to me that it was being spun from one tall dancer to another—and now a drum somewhere was going faster and faster—and the dancer's feet were following its beat—

"Oh that—we do it every year at Elverley Fair. Bit superstitious, I think. They say the barley harvest won't come if they don't do it. Then they say they don't believe in it really. But they all get worried if they think it isn't going to be done. And then there are other reasons that they won't say."

I looked at her properly and she looked away from me.

"What do you mean?" I asked. She had turned her head so that I could make out her expression again. She was being perfectly serious.

"What they won't say—I'm not s'posed to say, either. Tell you a few things. See the little dancer threading through them? That's the Brat! Some say the Brat is the harvest seed. One version is that the Brat must always come from Elverley. Another, that the Brat really comes from somewhere else. Been done for hundreds of years. I can do the Brat's dance."

She began hopping and crossing her legs to the beat of the music and she did it perfectly though she was grinning at me at the same time.

At that moment a man came round the back of the crowd. A bent old man, he had a tray supported by a string round his neck and had been—was—selling something. I could not make out what, in the dark. He had obviously spotted us because he came straight over in our direction. I wished he wouldn't because I did not want to spend any money. I could see him over her shoulder. He was calling through the music.

"Buy, buy the marigold. Elverley marigolds."

And then I saw him see her. He saw her dancing. I don't think he saw me at all. And it was as if he saw something he should not. He spun round on his heel and shuffled off back into the crowd, and the girl did not notice.

"Did you hear the woman singing, earlier on? She dances in the last bit, too—and that's the longest—all by herself. She's the one who runs it all and she's my mum. Come on—the last bit's just starting and it goes on forever."

I stared. I had never seen anything like it before, and now that I knew I wasn't lost I would have liked to have gone on watching it. But this girl had picked up my bag again, had grabbed my hand.

"We go this way," she told me.

We went.

We had no sooner turned our backs on the fair and the dancers than we were slipping through a wicket-gate in the churchyard wall and were cutting along a path between the graves and into the dark. I could hardly see where we were going. There were the big shapes of the yew trees to one side of us and the squat tower of the church on the other. It was too cloudy for stars. Underfoot the path was slippery with moss, and white slabs and battered crosses lay on either side.

"Walk behind me here," she ordered, letting go of my hand. "Path narrows. Hope you're not scared. I still think I'm going to be scared—and then it makes me laugh. Look out! Steps down here—four of them."

I let my feet find the steps first. It was more confusing than anything. I steadied myself on a big gravestone and wondered whose it was.

"You ought not to be carrying my stuff," I complained.

"I know the way," she replied. Her tone of voice indicated that she reckoned she could carry the bag with a good deal less trouble than I could. "But I'll need your help down with it when we get to the ha-ha."

"The what?" I asked, wondering if I had heard right. But that question got lost because we were going out through another gate that led down into a shadowy, steep-sided lane. She had a warm hand. I had noticed that she made sure of taking hold of my hand again. It was even darker down here. I decided I might as well hold her hand as if I meant it.

"Who are you?" I asked into the darkness.

"Thought perhaps I wouldn't tell," the voice teased. "Then you would have to wonder about me all the way down to Dockhurst's barn. But that's not fair, is it? I suppose I'm a bit like you now. I sort of visit Dockhurst sometimes. Oh, and my name's Chloe. . . . Well, I had to have a name, didn't I? C'mon, we go round here. If we cut across Mr. Bascombe's land and down over his ha-ha we save ourselves half a mile."

I was really only certain about the last bit.

"What *is* a ha-ha? Is it a joke or is it that it's really something else that you're not saying, Chloe?"

Chloe laughed.

"A ha-ha's a ha-ha! Mum's always called it a ha-ha and I've always called it a ha-ha. And Mr. Bascombe's got one. We'll get to it and then you'll know."

We seemed to have come out of the village and were walking along under a hedge. I couldn't hear her bare feet, only the crunch of my own shoes. All at once I found that she was steering us off the road.

"Through the gap here," she said in an undertone. "And keep your voice down because we're on private land here, just behind his house. His ha-ha's on the far side. And if old Bascombe's dog comes—you leave him to me."

That made me feel a bit uncomfortable. I didn't really know Chloe, yet I didn't want to not go with her. (I was lost without her now, anyway.) I wondered what we were letting ourselves in for.

"What sort of dog is it?" I whispered.

"It's a wolfhound—Irish wolfhound—lovely big thing," came back. "Bascombe lives alone—that's why he keeps it."

I supposed it was all right. Actually a large part of me didn't think it was all right at all. I couldn't help feeling it was a little bit off to walk through somebody else's garden, even if it was the middle of the night. I also had a rather clear memory of myself when small and a neighbor's Great Dane had accidentally got into our flat and chased me round and round and then up onto the kitchen table. It put me right off dogs, too, that had, for a long time. I didn't like to admit that I was still rather wary of large dogs, and, from what I could remember, Irish wolfhounds were just that. In fact, if I hadn't been in front of Chloe I would have been glad to turn back and walk that extra half mile.

"I think I can hear it," Chloe was saying. "Stand still a sec'. I wonder if Bascombe's chained it up."

I froze. I prayed that it was chained up. I prayed that Mr. Bascombe was on holiday and that neither he nor his dog were here at all. I remembered that Chloe was carrying my bag. We couldn't begin to run with that bag. I knew exactly what was inside it. And if we abandoned it, and if we did escape, we would have to admit what we had been up to, at least to Dockhurst, and I would never hear the end of it all week.

I stayed rooted to the spot. We were standing together, in complete darkness, in the middle of a lawn. There was an overpowering scent of wallflowers and my heart was banging in my ears.

A terrible baying came out of that darkness.

There was something particularly uncanny about it—it seemed to come from every direction at once. I would not have known in which direction to run, yet I so wanted to run. Chloe's hand tightened a little. I felt hot and cold at the same time.

"Don't move," Chloe whispered.

It must have got out from wherever it was. The baying got nearer and then I could hear the sound of a heavy dog bounding toward us from our right. I was only wishing that old Bascombe would come out and rescue us.

"Hello Paddy," Chloe called, with a maddening calm. "Paddy boy, here!"

She let go of my hand. She stepped forward.

"Paddy boy . . . come here!"

The hound stopped dead in its tracks in front of us. It must have seen her—heard her. I braced myself. Yet what was so astonishing was that the great baying gurgled down into a whimper. Its shadow twisted. . . .

The wolfhound was running away!

There was a scampering of feet off into the distance—and then an enormous silence.

I just stood there, feeling winded.

"Funny thing," Chloe was saying to me in a sad voice, "but once he always came to me when I called. Now he only runs from me." She sounded absurdly disappointed. I was thankful that she could not see my face. "C'mon," she said. "He may have woken Bascombe."

I was almost too choked with relief to speak. There were so many things to be relieved about. This man Bascombe coming out of the darkness to order us off his property would have been nothing. I did manage to pick up the bag and Chloe made no comment. We walked along, side by side. There was lots more lawn. I was just beginning to decide that I could see a little farther than I had thought when Chloe grabbed me by the wrist.

"Stop! Don't come any farther for a minute. Must let me find the ha-ha first."

I can remember being cross inside because she still hadn't told me what a ha-ha was. I could see Chloe going forward, and she seemed to be feeling for something with her foot, and then all at once she sat down in the grass.

"It's here," Chloe said. "Careful, if you come too far you'll go over. Sit by me, I'm on the edge. A ha-ha's a wall, but it's built down into a ditch so that it doesn't get in the way of the view. But we're on top of it, you see, so we've got to jump down. Then we're almost at the barn. I'll go first."

Before I could reply she had launched herself forward and disappeared from sight. It was as if she had just jumped out of this world. I heard her land with a grunt and a breaking of sticks but I could not see the bottom. Then I could just make out her hands reaching up. I reckoned it was at least a six-foot drop. I lowered my bag down to her. Bag and hands vanished in the shadow. I felt oddly absurd, sitting up top, legs dangling, bag gone, Chloe gone, and me not even knowing where I was, except that I knew I sat on an edge—of a ha-ha!

"Jump," said Chloe's voice.

So I jumped. I hoped I would land on my feet, I hoped I wouldn't turn an ankle. I seemed to fall endlessly.

I landed on Chloe. Chloe yelped and then there was the pair of us sprawling over each other in this rather damp bottom of the ha-ha. For an instant I could only lie with all the breath knocked out of me. I had the unreal feeling that I was not quite sure which were Chloe's arms and which were mine. At first I just lay, wondering if I were all right. Then I wondered if Chloe were all right. She was certainly warm. An insect ticked somewhere in the grass. Then I became alarmed because she seemed to be shaking all over —until I realized that she was laughing—in complete silence.

I asked her if she were okay.

"Me? We might have killed each other!" she said between gasps. And then she was laughing again. I found myself laughing, too—I wasn't quite sure why. "But are you all right?" she managed to get out. "All my idiot fault. You couldn't possibly have seen me."

She did not attempt to move. On second thought, perhaps she couldn't.

"I think I'm in one piece," I announced, half-crawling off her to find out. I was.

"Good thing you can't see me," she was saying out of the darkness. "Hair's full of leaves."

I could hear her straightening herself. Then I discovered my bag by falling over it.

"C'mon," she said. "I'd better deliver you. Up this bank and we're in the lane again."

I followed on her heels. It wasn't easy with my bag because even this other side was quite steep. Then we did come out onto the lane and everything was easier. We walked on a bit more under the black trees. The lane rounded a corner and, almost at once, there was a building.

"Here we are," Chloe told me. "That's Dockhurst's barn. Go round to the other side and you'll find the door. You'll have to knock. He's never fitted a bell."

"Aren't you coming, too?"

For a moment she did not seem to want to answer.

"Won't want to see me," she said, a little sadly.

"Oh!"

"Go on, Matt. He won't bite you."

"Well—thanks for bringing me."

She stood there in front of me a moment as if she were going to make some reply, a shadow in the dark lane. All at once she leaned forward and kissed me on the cheek—then she was gone. I was so surprised that I did not see which way she went. And there was no sound. I could not hear her. I supposed she was running barefoot along the roadside.

Again it was like . . . before I had ever seen her. It was silent and lonely. I turned away. I began to wonder if Dockhurst really was here. I carried my bag up toward the huge barn.

2

M ind how you behave while you're there," my
father had said. "Remember it will be his
house you'll be in."

At moments as I groped my way toward the barn
I was not certain whether I was walking on the path
or on the garden. I seemed to stumble the longest way
round before I actually found the door. It was so dark
that I had to feel for the knocker with my hand. There
was no knocker.

I knocked with my fist.

There was no answer.

Surely Dockhurst was not at the midnight fair—
perhaps he had gone there and had missed the coach
altogether? Or was Dockhurst asleep? I could see no
light. A horrible sinking feeling came down all over
me. Was this even Dockhurst's barn?

But then why should Chloe have brought me here?

The door had a handle. I twisted it, not expecting it to open, and almost fell inside.

There was a very thick curtain just inside the door. This was no hay barn, anyway. I had to grope my way through the curtain. Then I had an enormous feeling of relief.

I was in one gigantic room. At the very farthest end there was just one small island of light. Dockhurst was sitting in the center of it, his back toward me, a drawing board on his knees. That was all I could see. What was he doing? Was he all right?

I drew a deep breath.

"Dockhurst," I said.

Dockhurst did not hear.

I staggered forward, grazing my shin against something, and dropped my bag. It was then that I realized how tired I was. I just stood there, my shin hurting like mad. At least I had made Dockhurst turn round.

The man revolved on his seat, though still crouching over the board on his knees. He sat peering out into the darkness where I stood.

"Who are you?" he wanted to know.

I felt almost too dopey to answer. I could only register that Dockhurst was as Dockhurst had always seemed to be.

"Oh, you are *you!* Blazes, boy, it's old Matt and no other." The man's voice was a growl but I was used to his growling. I even managed to grin, just listening to him. "So I'm late, am I, boy? That's it, is it? Working—that's what I'm still doing. Work's an illness, Matt. Mind you catch it. Never any cure—that's its whole beauty. But you—you found your own way here in the dark? My other friends all lose theirs in the light! How, under the breath of heaven, did you get here?"

"Chloe brought me," I managed to say. "Didn't you know?"

"*Who* brought you? *Chloe* brought you?" Somehow Dockhurst found somewhere in the shadows to put down his drawing board and got up onto his feet. He was a short and powerful man.

"That's right," I agreed. "She saw me after I got off the coach." I remember yawning.

"Chloe brought you," Dockhurst muttered, almost to himself. "What would you have known about Chloe? But it would have been so like Chloe." He looked up. "You see, boy—I told nobody that you were coming. Wasn't their business. Don't talk much when I'm working. But the village always talks. Your Chloe, now—tell me. Girl about your own age, yes? If I tell you that she had red hair, bare feet . . . liked her own way . . ."

It was like listening to someone talking from very far away. I was very sleepy.

"I couldn't really see the color of her hair," I admitted, "but that was her."

Dockhurst strode away into the darkness of his barn. "Just like you and me, boy," he laughed. "All cats have the same color in a coal cellar—with the light off!" There was a clicking of switches and the whole of Dockhurst's studio was ablaze with light.

When I could take my hands from my eyes I could see how big the barn was. Down one side there was a stretch of canvas nearly fifteen feet long, more like a piece of scenery for a stage than a picture. It was already half-covered with dancers, dancers in white masks and long cloaks, carrying torches, and with a high bonfire in the middle. I noticed the one small dancer again, the one dancer without a mask, a dancer alone, turning a cartwheel. I could see whole racks of pictures at the other end, pictures stacked one against the other, and then a table littered with tubes of color, dirty rags, and two great pots full of brushes. There were sketches, photographs, and posters pinned around the walls (Dockhurst's posters—and photographs that had given Dockhurst ideas). There was an unmade bed, a stack of newspapers on the floor, and a towering bookcase stuffed with different-colored books. I had always imagined the barn to be something like this—but I had not realized that it would be so big.

"And with just one snap of the lights," Dockhurst announced, "just a cat becomes a red cat, a blue cat, a green, or a white. You've never seen a green cat, have you, boy? No, neither have I. But it did not stop me painting one once. Show you sometime, if ever I manage to find it. Now, what am I here to look for this time? Yes! Now tell me if you recognize this one? It was the red hair that fascinated me when doing it."

I smiled. I could not help but wake up a little while watching, talking, and listening to Dockhurst.

"Now you should be yelling at me for not being at your coach stop—and you'd be right—but to me I'm still in the middle of the afternoon." He was pulling his picture out from the stack. Then he carried it over to a chair, had to lift off a box of chalks, three battered books, and another old rag, before he could finally set his picture up. "Come and look at red hair, Matt." And then he was diving down into an immense portfolio and rummaging in it.

I looked at the picture on the chair. I looked at it—and was jolted awake. For a moment I could not be sure if I was more startled by *how* Dockhurst had painted her—rather than *whom* he had painted. I only knew what an awful lot I would have to learn before I could even begin to see . . . let alone draw or paint in the way that Dockhurst could. Yet I could see that, more marvelously than any photograph could have done, Dockhurst had captured her.

"That's Chloe!" I exclaimed.

Looking at his picture, at the slashes of browns and greens, the splurge of blue, and all the different reds—they meant nothing—and then you blinked your eyes and they became Chloe standing. You looked down at her from above and there was this mass of red hair down her back. She was standing on a green riverbank in the sunshine and had only just come out of the water. She was twisting round and looking up at me over her shoulder, laughing and putting out her tongue. There were freckles all over her face, a blue towel in her hand. Yet she, the river, the towel, and the riverbank were only tiny marks of different-colored paint, streak and splodge and spot.

"Never could get her to keep still," Dockhurst was grumbling. "Had to work from memory. Did it . . . did it for her mother originally. Somehow, the thing never got given. There was a reason. So it's still here. Look—this is Chloe, too. Different! Hardly anybody knows I ever did that."

He put a yellowing sheet of paper into my hand, not very large, and rough at the edges. This was just a drawing. There was no color. And yet it held my attention. I took the drawing in my hand. It was somehow cold and still.

There were no boldly blocked-in shapes, there was no sense of movement here. The whole of this drawing was meant to be motionless and it was all done so delicately, with hardly more than a single outline by a perfectly controlled pencil. It was Chloe's face only, a Chloe who did not move, who must surely have been asleep. The eyes were closed and the mouth unsmiling.

"That was Chloe," Dockhurst said blankly. Then he looked back at his painting and nodded to himself. "That's how she was. She used to do a lot of swimming. The drawing though, that should have been the last."

He took his drawing back. I did not understand him. He stood there, swaying a little, staring at his own work. All at once he remembered that I was there.

"Want anything to eat, boy—or drink? You put me off my stroke. But then of course . . . I should have met you myself." He scratched the back of his tangled gray hair.

"I—I'd be quite happy just to go to bed," I confessed. The mere thought brought back my yawns again.

"Hey! Of course you're tired. Would be! Who's chatting and yapping now? Show you to your room. *I* sleep down here." He waved in the direction of the unmade bed. "Don't expect you to. Guest rooms are up the ladder behind you. I'll take your bag. Up you go—hand over hand. Sure you don't want anything to drink?"

I was sure. It was like climbing up into a ship.

It was a long, high white room that Dockhurst had left me in. I suppose there were no pictures up there because all the walls sloped in with the roof of the barn. My bed was down one side, covered with a bright red blanket. There was an enormously long dressing table and a row of built-in wardrobes. There was even a basin over in the far corner.

I dragged off my shirt and just let it drop onto the floor. I was deciding that I wouldn't be taking too long over washing. Yet I found that I was really too tired to be quick and that I was very dirty from falling down the ha-ha. So in fact I had to do rather a lot of washing. I have a memory of wearily leaning over that basin, at last cleaning my teeth, rather aware of a cool draught playing on my bare back and just thankful to be finishing. I swilled down the basin and finally turned round to bed.

Vaguely I registered that my bed was neatly turned down. I had no memory of having laid out my pajamas on the end. I saw my shirt hanging over the chair. I stopped!

Chloe was sitting on the dressing table, her legs dangling, and she was still very grubby from falling down the ha-ha. She was busy brushing more leaves out of her hair . . . with my hairbrush. I suppose I was stupidly tired. Somehow I only seemed to be able to realize that Dockhurst had been quite right—her hair really was as red as that.

I remember her saying, "This is the room I like staying in the most." She seemed to say it to herself, not to me at all. She did not even look at me.

Somehow and illogically, I was not really surprised to see her—not today, not tonight. Everything had been so different today . . . but I was just too tired.

"What have you come for?" I found myself asking.

She did look at me then.

"It's my room, really," she told me. "Like to come back and look at it sometimes. Came to see you, too, though. I forgot to ask you something."

I blinked. Nobody seemed to want to let me go to bed.

"You'll see me," Chloe said, "—on the green tomorrow, in the morning, by the river. So you're coming out to look for me."

It sounded more like telling me than asking me. Not that I was in any mood to argue.

"Yes—if you like—if Dockhurst doesn't want me."

"He won't," Chloe announced with conviction. "He's started a new picture. You'll be lucky if he even remembers you're here. But I shall remember."

"Does Dockhurst know *you're* here?"

She shook her head and pointed. Behind me was the window, wide open.

"How did you get in?" I asked, not really understanding.

"Ladder perhaps," Chloe said mysteriously. "You don't have to look so worried. I won't kill myself. My mum doesn't know I'm here either. Going to say—I like those pajamas. All those reds. Aren't you going to put them on, Matt? I've been admiring them ever since I put them out."

I was not too sure that I would.

Chloe seemed to think this was funny.

"No? Look—I've another idea."

In a flash she was off the dressing table and had snatched up my new pajamas. She was crouching—she was putting out her tongue.

"Tell you what—I'll give you your jacket back tomorrow, on the green. How's that? You'll have to come out and look for me now."

It came to me that I was being distinctly out-maneuvered.

"Hey—give that back," I demanded.

I made to grab at her but she was all hands. Then she had jumped up onto the bed and before I knew what was happening my own pajama trousers were being thrust over my face. I couldn't see a thing. I was beating the air. I also seemed to be losing the pants I had on and Chloe was laughing.

I had to laugh, too—in spite of myself. I backed away from her, grabbed at my pants, then managed to get my pajama trousers off my ears. . . .

I was laughing all to myself.

Chloe had gone.

I supposed I would just have to go and look for her on the green now. I supposed I would have to tell Dockhurst why, as well. I went over to the big window and stared out into the dark. The night air was against my face and all I could see were the distant lights of the village. I had to admire the way Chloe had turned the tables on me. It was only after I had lowered the window a bit that I began to wonder what she had done with the ladder.

3

Even before I opened my eyes I had that feeling of sunshine. Red light glowed through my eyelids, was warm on my bare shoulder. I savored the thought of where I must be before I opened my eyes. I stretched to my full length and then my feet found that someone was sitting on the end of my bed. Cautiously, I withdrew my feet a little. My nose was being tickled by something soft!

I opened my eyes rather abruptly.

I was staring upward. Now I could see that I had a soaring ceiling of wide white-painted boards sloping up on either side of me like a high white tent. My nose was being tickled by the end of a very long paintbrush. It was Dockhurst who was sitting on my bed—in an old yellow shirt.

"Cup of tea?" Dockhurst growled, without any smile, more like a threat than an offer.

I sat up, I smiled, tried to snatch the brush and was foiled. Then Dockhurst did smile. The whole bedroom was filled with sunshine because the sloping window had no curtains. There was a great chatter of birds outside. I had slept well. Dockhurst had brought a tray, with a teapot and cups and biscuits. I lay there, taking it all in, hearing myself say good morning.

Dockhurst poured tea.

"Tell you what we're doing today," he announced. "All this morning—I am going to work. First thing—so are you. You begin by sitting still. Can you sit still? I'm starting my work on you."

So there I was, sitting up—sipping tea when I thought I could get away with it. And there was Dockhurst running his pencil over a sheet of gray paper, snatching a gulp himself in between.

"After this," Dockhurst continued, "I'm cooking us a man-sized breakfast and then, while we're eating it, I am going to take a look at what you've been doing since I last saw your work." His head looked up from his gray paper. "You've brought some of your work with you?"

I nodded. I had promised to bring some of my own work and I had brought it—but I was not looking forward too much to what Dockhurst might say about it. People had been kind enough to say my work was quite good, but Dockhurst would be very much harder to impress. That I knew.

"I have brought . . . two of my sketchbooks. I expect you'll call me out about some of it."

Dockhurst carried on drawing.

"I expect I will," he said.

27

So I tried to sit still. All in a rush I was remembering I had to see Chloe this morning and wondered how I could ask.

"You don't have to sit all tight like that," Dockhurst said suddenly, his paw sweeping out for his cup. "*You* ought to know that. And just drink your tea when you feel like drinking your tea, think just as you like to think—and sit!"

I suppose that I should have known—not that Dockhurst had ever tried to draw me before. I thought of Dockhurst's drawings of Chloe and wished that I could draw like that. I wondered what he would make of my things.

"After breakfast—and after I have called you out—you are not going to watch me draw, and I'm not going to watch you. Don't move! Don't mind you drinking your tea when you like as long as you don't move. After breakfast—you are not going to draw at all. You are going to walk round Elverley—looking. Looking, boy, because all drawing is looking—and then other people look at the marks your brain has made because you have been looking. So looking will be your job today. But I shan't want you to draw what you see—not this time. Not yet. Meanwhile I am going to be old and selfish and spend the morning getting on with my work. And then we'll meet at twelve for bread and cheese. How's that?"

I decided that this was a chance to put my teacup down.

"What do you want me to look at when I go round Elverley?"

"You'll find that out when I ask you afterward —over lunch. But this I will tell you. Our skills

—yours and mine—well, I'll tell you what most of my artist friends won't ever admit." He scratched his head with the end of his pencil. "Drawing has become like riding and sailing. Sort of sport. No need for it now. Once the world needed so many people to draw and paint. It was the only way to give other people an idea as to what other things looked like. Then came the camera. That took the artist's bread-and-butter work away. But never despise photography, boy. No one can appreciate it more than we do—because we have been trained to look. Yet we can do something no photographer can manage. Do you know what that is? We can take what we see and pour it through our minds before we let it out again, changed—much or little—but changed, Matt, by what we know and are."

I ate a biscuit and wondered about eating another one. I remember wondering if I should be careful not to put myself off that man-sized breakfast.

Dockhurst, I reckoned, could make anything feel changed, simply by talking about it. When Dockhurst drew Chloe, though, it wasn't Chloe herself; it was Dockhurst seeing Chloe. So what was Chloe herself? She had been right enough about Dockhurst. He was going to do his own work this morning and so it was going to be possible to see Chloe. And after all, wasn't Chloe herself a part of Elverley? I remembered that she was the reason I was sitting up here without a pajama jacket—she'd pinched it. All at once I realized that I ought to be answering Dockhurst. But the man had already gone back to drawing me. He hadn't noticed. He was working.

"Dockhurst, do we get changed, too—by what we draw?"

For some moments the pencil went on moving relentlessly over the gray paper.

"Always," he replied. "And I'll tell you something else. So do other people—if they will only look."

He went on working. I reached back for my tea and contrived to finish it.

"Dockhurst?"

The man did not seem to hear.

"Dockhurst, does Chloe come here often?"

The pencil stopped then. But Dockhurst did not look up—rather, more down.

"She used to be here—very often."

"But not now?"

"I do still see her here," he admitted, "but only sometimes."

It was a glorious morning.

It was a glorious morning.

Dockhurst had stood over me and made quite certain that I did not take even my smallest sketchbook, and not even a pencil stub.

"I can tell you, too, that the village shop won't sell you a ballpoint either—on my orders."

I wondered what Dockhurst had told them. After all, they did not know me. It was going to be a bit hard if another strange boy went into the shop today. It was a bit hard on me. I remembered Dockhurst's having said that nobody in the village even knew about my arrival, and I was puzzled. Not that I was worried.

Dockhurst had almost run back to his work, and I crunched happily away down the path and on to the road. I would walk comfortably round to the village and not through old Bascombe's garden. This time I would at least be able to see where I was going.

It was still quite early. Dockhurst had in fact got us up very early. The air had a sparkle to it, the hedges rose high and green on either side, and there was a lot of chirruping from the birds. From the path I could not see the village at all. A small stream was running by the roadside, bubbling and jollying over stones. In the distance I heard a bell striking—it was the clock on the Elverley Church tower—its chiming resonating over the fields.

Over breakfast, Dockhurst had looked at all the drawings in both my sketchbooks. All along—ever since it had been suggested that I should come—it had been a bit alarming to think what Dockhurst would say about them. But I had also been afraid there wouldn't be enough to show him. It had been his suggestion that I should try to do some on my own. He had teased me into drawing with him when we had gone out together on his visits and he had already taught me a bit. At least, he had taught me to enjoy it. So Dockhurst had sat munching toast—to my surprise, breakfast was served on a smart white table-cloth, in spite of the mess in the rest of the barn—and seemed to be able to look at both sketchbooks at one and the same time.

One was used to Dockhurst looking at things upside down or sideways or with only one eye. When he'd invited me down, he had told me some of the things he wanted me to sketch: a milk bottle, and then the same milk bottle with a rose stuck in it; three walnuts, and those same three walnuts with a clean white handkerchief spread over them; the view from my bedroom window at night and the same view the next day; the budgerigar cage without the budgerigar. . . .

"They don't sound too exciting, boy—but oh, you will find them difficult. You'll hate me for giving 'em and that'll be fine. You'll be supposed to hate me."

He was right. I hated him most satisfactorily. But I didn't have the face not to try. I knew I was coming down to see him—and I liked him. I found I didn't get bored. (My dad had thought I wouldn't stick at it!) I even went through a stage of getting swellheaded about my efforts. But in front of Dockhurst I was petrified.

First Dockhurst said nothing. He did wrinkle up his nose at everything—but then Dockhurst was always wrinkling up that nose of his. He did not even take me to task when he came to commenting. He even grinned.

"Got a nasty feeling, Matt, you might almost have enjoyed yourself doing some of this. Have to put a stop to that. That's why your next job's thinking about what you might draw, in Elverley, and telling me your reason. For a start, remember what you see. Want you to spend the morning drawing without doing any drawing. Asking you to move an imaginary pencil in your real head."

He wouldn't say if anything I had done was either good or bad.

The road took a steep slope down and at the bottom the stream emptied into a pond that lay at the near end of a field, while the road itself swung away round a blind corner. I suppose I must have walked right by Bascombe's land. There were geese on the pond. I stood there, watching them in an idle sort of way. After all, wasn't I supposed to stop and watch?

The surface of the pond was not like the stream —it was glass-still. The geese, gray necked and dark winged, just floated on green water without seeming to do anything at all. The field beyond stretched far and away toward a wood. Flies buzzed up at my face and I could taste the smell of cow.

A bicycle bell shrilled sharply.

I jumped—almost the wrong way.

A man in a dapper, dark suit, bushy eyebrows, and a rector's dog collar, a tall man astride a tall bicycle that still seemed a size too small, was pedaling madly down toward me. It was one of those old-fashioned bikes with a basket on the front, and the basket was full.

"Helloooo Maaatt!" a huge hollow voice shouted as the man negotiated both curve and me at an alarming angle, the long-trousered knees pumping up and down as he charged the farther slope.

I stared at his now retreating back. I was obviously no secret in Elverley. Then I marched on up the hill the other way, wondering what it was I was going to see.

Round and up and between more trees, and I was passing cottages that seemed weighed down into the ground by the thatch upon their roofs. My lane narrowed and I saw other cottages higher up the hillside. Then I was passing the churchyard again and even with a bright sun shining it was dark under its trees. Just ahead was the green.

Nobody seemed to be about. I saw the remains of the fair—the empty booths and stalls, the round circle of white ash where the bonfire had been. I paused before crossing the road to let a post-office van go by. The postman waved.

Can't be me, I thought—but there was no one else.

Dock had certainly disarmed me. Without my sketchbook, pencils, charcoal, I could not just sit and let the world know that I was a budding artist, that Mr. Dockhurst himself was teaching me, and that anyway I was rather good. Instead, I had to do real work. I had to look.

I wondered which way to go. Chloe could hardly have arrived yet—it was too early. I decided that I would at least find my way round the green, so I set off across it. The village seemed to go only halfway round. Beyond, there was just more countryside. I looked back. There were the hills down which the coach had come. It was only when I had walked quite a little way that I saw the river on the green's farther side. I stopped and looked back again. The village houses looked almost like toys. I decided that I might as well walk down to the river. I wondered where Chloe would find me—or where I would find Chloe.

Someone was picking marigolds along the river-bank, armfuls of marigolds. Even from a distance I could see that it was not Chloe. It was a woman . . . a middle-aged woman with streaky iron-gray hair, moving slowly, picking as she went. I remember that she had on a yellow blouse and that it was a shade of yellow different from the marigolds. I watched her as I walked. She was picking her way toward me, bent over among the flowers, not looking up.

I wondered if I had arrived at a good place to stop. I was where the river arrived beside the green. Perhaps this was where Chloe meant to meet me. Or should I just go on? There was no pressing reason to do anything in particular. I simply went on walking.

As I approached, the woman straightened her back. I found myself drawing in a breath. I knew that in the country everybody said good morning. She looked at me very fair and square. I wondered if I ought to speak first.

I wasn't given any opportunity.

"Oh, Matt dear, will you take these from me so that I can come up the bank?"

She spoke as if she had always known me. It was a tone of voice one couldn't really question. I went down the bank and took the heap of flowers from her. She still showed traces in her gray hair that it had once been red. Her face had lots of little lines and tiny freckles and she was smiling up at me.

". . . Suppose he didn't remember to tell you?"

"Tell me?" I heard myself ask, still taken aback and not quite grasping what she was talking about.

"He was supposed to warn you against swimming in the Elverley River. Oh—it's so obvious he forgot. And shouldn't you at least have brought a pencil and paper with you?"

"Dockhurst—Mr. Dockhurst—he said I could only go out and *look*, to begin with."

She could certainly grasp what I was talking about.

"Oh yes, Matt. He would. That is exactly . . . Dockhurst. He is . . . was . . . I suppose you could say he's a very old friend of mine. But he will forget what's important. So I shall have to ask you to promise me—I know it is a warm day—promise me you won't slide off to have a swim."

She was still smiling but I could see that she did mean what she said.

"Why no," I assured her, "I haven't got any bathing things, have I?"

The woman nodded, directed that we climb the bank, gripped my shoulder, and came up with me. At the top I gave her the marigolds back.

"Our little river has this strong current that never ceases," she told me. "And then there are the weeds. Weeds catch your feet, current pulls you down. I only tell you . . . a girl was lost in this river like that. It must be nearly eight years ago now."

I nodded. Eight years seemed rather a long time to me. I wondered who this woman was.

"I always collect marigolds at this time of year, while they are at their best. They are to remember her by, because she liked them so much. I enjoy remembering her—but that doesn't mean to say I want to have to collect them for you, too. You see, you might not realize how powerful our river is. It comes down over a weir—that's the reason. The awful thing was . . . it should never have happened. . . . She knew our river so well."

"Where—where is the weir?" I asked, feeling that this might change the subject a little.

"See our hills at the back? Then those two higher ones—in the middle?"

She pointed, a bunch of marigolds still in her pointing hand.

"Down here we call them the Elverley mounds,

because that's what they look like. But when you get up there you will find that they are a plateau really. The edge of the Elverley Moor. It goes on for miles—mostly sheep, with a forest down the center, where the river runs. The weir is on the edge. It's a marvelous sight, Matt—all that water flowing over the lip of the weir. You can stand on a narrow wooden footbridge right above it and watch the river pour and pour down between the rocks beneath your feet. Dockhurst did a whole series of paintings of it once—but he won't go there nowadays."

"I'm staying at his barn," I said. "I've seen a lot of his work there."

"His barn? Yes—I was the one who found that for him, originally. He so wanted . . . it was so important for him to have his own place where he could do his work in peace. At first we had a cottage by the rectory. Then we had that barn turned into his studio. It was perfect for him then. . . ."

The woman looked up from her remembering.

"I've been in Elverley a very long time," she told me.

There was a silence.

"Then—then you must know why they dance on the Elverley green?"

"Oh—so you've heard of that, have you? You haven't seen us dancing, I suppose?"

"Yes, I have. I watched last night when I got off the coach. But only for a moment because . . . afterward, somebody told me it was a superstition. Why do you think they do it?"

"So you did see some of it. I was dancing myself. It's not what I call a superstition. We do it—because it has always been done. There's a rightness about it. It marks the year. It gives a shape to life, like saying good morning and good-bye. It's what was done and is done and shall be done. That is a good thing. Dockhurst once painted us dancing. I remember that his picture almost frightened me—and yet I was grateful for it, because it showed me that we both knew why the dancers danced. We don't always agree, Dockhurst and I, but we both understand why I dance, why the whole village must come to the dance—and perhaps why he does not have to dance. For Dockhurst—it is enough to see. I . . . I can remember being taught the steps, Matt, by my old Gran. She knew how it should be done, even when she could hardly drag one foot in front of the other herself. But I remember her old eyes glittering while she taught me, and her fist would beat out the time . . . and I learned all the songs from her, in the old words. Gran used to sing as if her heart was going to overflow. So sad they were, you see. My mother used to teach me, too, but in quite a different way, usually when we were doing something between us and at some unexpected time. Yet when my mother sang those songs—then they seemed more angry than sad. But brave, too. . . . Sometimes, I sing them like that."

All at once she turned away. She moved her marigolds to her other arm.

"You won't swim, will you, Matt? Now, these days, I don't go down to Dockhurst's very much, but I expect we shall see each other again. You can . . . give Dockhurst my regards. Enjoy your stay with him. Tell him to send you across to me—I'll sing you some of the songs as they should be, as they used to be, and as they're going to be. And you must show me your drawings."

She was walking away. I did not even have a chance to say good-bye. It was only afterward that I realized she had been calling me by my name and yet had not once mentioned who she was.

4

The river curved away from the green and through broad meadows. There was a stile, and I half climbed over and then sat there, looking back toward the village. I could just make out a huge fuel truck edging its length cautiously round the church, the sun flashing for an instant on its curved windscreen as it turned.

The sun was warmer now. The only person I could see was the woman carrying her flowers, who was now only a dot on the far side of the green. I remember deciding to explore the church on my way back. Churches could have marvelous carvings, gargoyles, tombs, and banners. Dockhurst was bound to ask me questions about it. And it would be a good place to draw if it rained.

Across the river an old dappled cart horse was getting down to some serious eating, its white mane flopped forward between its ears, its long face with the blue spottings on its nose slightly on one side as it cropped the long grass. I watched the line of its neck as it moved—and the heavy white fetlocks were like great muffs above the giant hooves. The horse took its time, lifting its head now and then to shake away the black persistent flies.

It was a chance to get on with more looking. I wondered if the village shop really would refuse to sell me a pen or even a pencil. Despite what Dockhurst had said, everyone I'd met thus far did seem to know who I was.

I watched a blue dragonfly planing over the reeds. From somewhere behind me there was a splashing in the river. I realized that somebody must be swimming, though, glancing back, I could not see who it was because of a bend in the river. Perhaps if I went on I would see who it was. It gave me a moment of purpose. I swung a leg over the stile and walked on round the path.

The river widened at the bend. There were high clumps of reeds and bulrushes but in one or two places the bank did slope down gently with grass and marigolds. I stood there, partly drugged with the warmth of the sun and not really surprised to see that the swimmer was Chloe.

The girl had not noticed me for she was wading out of the river on the farther side. Yet there was no doubt it was Chloe, even if she had tied up her hair and was still waist-deep in the water. I was almost treading on her clothes, bundled in a blue towel with white stripes, and as I bent to brush off some dirt I saw, right in the middle and neatly rolled, my scarlet pajama jacket. I straightened up, wondering what Chloe was doing and watching her.

It was the cart horse. Chloe was scrambling up the opposite bank, water running off her, a huge handful of grass in her fist.

"Sam!" her voice called high above the water. "Sam, Sam! Come on, Samuel—you know me."

I could see the cart horse. It was raising its head at her call.

"Sam! Sam!"

She was plunging toward the cart horse out of the rushes. Then all at once it had seen her. To my surprise its ears went back, it snorted, and with a whirl of heavy hooves, it turned about. I saw earth flying in the air, and, with a clumping gallop, it was away. Chloe was left standing, left holding her grass and looking rather forlorn. From where I stood, rather higher than Chloe, I could see that the cart horse was still running.

"Oooh!" Chloe wailed. I could hear it from my side.

I opened my mouth to speak, and then closed it. Should I call over to her—or should I wait? I stepped back a pace or two to be out of sight behind the taller rushes. But then I could not see Chloe either. She was still gazing sadly after the horse.

"Hi! C-h-l-o-e!"

She turned about at that, was seeing me at once, had dropped her grass and was waving. Her face burst into smiles.

"Hello! You *are* early! Didn't 'spect you yet. I'll come back over."

42

"Dockhurst gets up so early," I was shouting in explanation.

But she was already splashing down into the water, half tumbling, half wading through weed, then breaking into a half-dozen powerful strokes, and then wading once again. I saw how she kept her head well up to avoid wetting her hair. I went down and held out a hand that she obviously did not really need but did take. She splashed out and stood in front of me shaking a strand of weed off one foot. There was another bit that she was perfectly capable of removing, but I took it off for her.

"I've been told what a dangerous river this is," I teased. I also went and fetched her towel.

"It's not dangerous here," she said scornfully. "Nobody could drown here. It's farther upstream that you have to look out, where there's a weir. Going over that isn't so funny."

I handed her the blue towel. She liked being looked after.

"What made the horse bolt?" I asked.

"Oh, the horse." She began to dry her shoulders. "Did you see it, then? That was Sam. He used to let me do anything with him. I used to ride round the field on him. Of course, Sam's so broad you do rather have to do the splits. But I don't know, perhaps he's got old. . . . He doesn't really like me now. D'you know, I remember, ages ago, creeping out one night and riding him round in the dark—just for a dare with myself."

It wasn't difficult to imagine.

"Would you," I asked, "would you have ridden him again just now—if he had let you?"

"Might have. Came for a swim really—before meeting you. But I'm so glad you have come so early. We can have a gorgeous morning. Hey, d'you want to go in for a swim? I'll go in again."

I hadn't really expected that. For an instant I found myself calculating that it probably was quite dangerous unless you really knew what you were doing, and I might not show up too well in front of Chloe, who was probably a very good swimmer (so many girls were), and anyway . . .

"I haven't brought any things with me," I pointed out.

"Who cares? There's nobody around. Here—let's go and have a look."

She was climbing up the bank and actually looking, too.

"But I've got no towel," I protested.

"You can sit in the sun. I've done that before now. And there isn't anybody about. Come on in with me, it's so lonely doing things on one's own always." She had thrown her towel down and was making her way back to the water.

I stood there, remembering the gray-haired woman picking all those marigolds. There were marigolds everywhere.

"Aren't you coming?" Chloe was asking me over her shoulder. She was already paddling in.

It was hot, I told myself. I had to decide, I told myself. I knew already that I was shy, and shy because I wasn't confident. So I just went stubborn all over.

"No," I said.

So there she stood in the water, knee-deep. There was a strong current flowing too, I could see that. I could also see that I had hurt her a bit and I hadn't wanted to hurt her. After all there couldn't be much danger because there were the two of us here. I wondered if perhaps I ought to go in with her.

"I've also come out here because Dockhurst sent me," I said out loud. It must have sounded a bit hollow. "You never said we were going to swim."

"Didn't know then," Chloe pointed out. "You could always dry out on your pajama jacket."

"But what were we going to do this morning?" I was changing the subject. Deliberately, I bent down and rescued my jacket from the middle of her things. She watched me doing it.

"I only wanted to talk . . . really. I feel so lonely by myself. And I like Dockhurst and you like Dockhurst and so I thought we would have things to talk about. There were never many people in the village who liked to talk to him seriously—not about what he does. He says you even draw a bit. I—I can't much, but I feel at home with people who do, and don't laugh at it."

To my relief she was coming out of the water. She was picking up her towel again. She even wanted to talk about things I knew rather than me doing things she knew. And then—seeing her stand like that on the riverbank—all at once I knew exactly where I had seen her just like that before.

"You should never give up trying to draw," I told her. "Most people can learn." (I was echoing Dockhurst there.) "That's why I'm supposed to be walking round Elverley and just looking at it this morning. Not drawing, just looking. Dockhurst believes in looking at everything first. But you must know that.

45

Couldn't you take me round? You must know what there really is to see."

She was standing on one leg and had put a hand on my shoulder to steady herself while she dried her left foot. Suddenly she managed to become both pleased and doubtful at the same time. She overbalanced and put her foot down again a little unexpectedly.

"Of course I know. But me take you round Elverley? In the daytime? Now?"

"Yes," I said, wondering why she should find this difficult.

"S'pose I could," she admitted, as if it took a lot of thinking about. "Be rather a dare. You see—" she looked up, "I don't go to the village all that much."

"I—I thought you lived there."

She changed feet and I had to stand firm again.

"I come from—well, it's farther over really, now."

My face was very close to the red hair.

"Yet it must have been here that Dockhurst painted you," I pointed out.

She stopped her drying.

"He's shown that to you?"

There was a note in her voice that almost suggested that it was extraordinary that Dockhurst should have shown it at all.

"Yes. He showed it to me. I think it's marvelous!"

She looked at me patiently, as if she had heard all this said before.

"He can make anything look marvelous," she said slowly. "That's just what Dockhurst does. No—he didn't really paint me here. He just sort of did sketches and the painting itself he did back at the barn. D'you think it's me, though?"

"Of course it's you. It *is* you. He couldn't have begun to do it if you weren't the way you are. Wish I could begin to capture what he manages to capture. I'd love to be able to work like him."

"But d'you think I'm marvelous?" She sounded both serious and curious at the same time, as if she had never thought about the possibility before and really wanted to know.

"A picture only grabs half a split second," I told her. (That was Dockhurst again.) "But it's you that's all-round, all-alive, and all-real. You're what it's all about. No picture is as good as you are yourself."

Yet Chloe didn't seem to be convinced.

"People used to visit his barn and look much more at my pictures than at me. And Dock was so bad-tempered when he did this one. Everything was wrong and was my fault. I had to stand *here*. Well almost—no, there, just beyond where you're standing. And he wouldn't even let me dry."

She jumped down the bank to the correct place, twisted herself round and looked back up at me. She even held the towel just as she had in her picture.

"He made me stand still for ages."

"You had your hair down," I pointed out.

She nodded. I seemed to have done the right thing by remembering. It was as if it proved to her that I really had been struck by Dockhurst's picture of her. She tugged at the blue headband round her hair and shook it back.

Looking at her now, I had to admit to myself that it was also Dockhurst I was admiring.

"That's it," I said to her. "But you've got to move a bit more round."

She did move round, just as I directed. She stood absolutely right—and then she put her tongue out.

"You order me around like Dock," she accused, but she was laughing. All at once she was up beside me and scrabbling among her clothes. A comb came out of the middle of them. She began to comb out her red hair. "And I really do look as good as my picture?" she badgered.

I nodded. I was smiling back even though I was feeling peeved inside that I had been forbidden to bring my sketchbook. I could at least have tried to draw Chloe. Of course Dockhurst could have shown her standing like that with just a few pencil strokes. I watched how she was throwing her weight forward onto her right foot. . . .

She threw down her comb.

"Do you really want me to take you round Elverley?"

"Mmmmmm."

"All right. It's a dare. Might take you. There'll have to be a condition. . . ."

"What do you mean?"

With a toss of her head she flicked her hair forward so that she was peering at me through the strands—but she didn't answer directly.

"Never you mind. Got to think about that. Have to get my things on first. You sit over *there*. And talk to me while I'm doing it. Go on."

So I sat a little awkwardly and looked away, out across the river. The cart horse seemed to have settled down again. Chloe simply stood where she was in the marigolds and continued drying.

"You're not talking," she complained.

"What do you want me to talk about?"

"You have to choose that—otherwise you're not doing the talking."

I supposed she was right. I noticed out of the corner of my eye that she had half wriggled out of her black swimsuit—and here was me without even a sketchbook. I saw how her freckles trickled right down her back.

"You're still not saying very much," she said over her shoulder.

"Chloe?" I asked in a rush.

"Yes."

"What's the real reason for the dancing on Elverley green?"

"Not supposed to tell you that." Her voice was coming through her T-shirt now. She was finding it quite a business steering all that hair through the neck.

"Is—is it a secret, then?" I asked the waving green shirt.

Chloe's eyes emerged.

"Very secret. Could tell you, though. Just like I could take you round the village."

"Will you?"

"Matt. There is a place I want you to take me to."

"Where's that?"

"Want you to come to the weir with me," Chloe said.

I could not see her face. For a moment I was able to see where round her stern she had no freckles at all. I went back to looking across the river.

"Isn't the weir up in the Elverley mounds?" I asked.

"Mmmm. Have to go up there, sometimes. It's very lonely—when you get that far."

Somehow, Chloe being lonely, Chloe being really lonely, had not struck me before. I looked back at her. All at once I was imagining her being not quite so confident, but me there as well, as a sort of compensation.

"I'll come with you—if Dockhurst lets me."

"He'll let you. If I ask him, he'll let you."

I supposed Dockhurst would. I supposed Dockhurst would laugh at me. It wasn't going to matter if he did. I watched Chloe finish dressing and fold up her wet swimsuit in her towel.

"C'mon," she said. "Like me to carry your pajama jacket with my things?"

I decided that I would carry my own jacket.

We did not go straight back across the green to Elverley. Chloe preferred to lead me another way round, by the river's edge, under a long line of willows. It was like slipping into the village by the back door. We came round the end of a hedgerow and all at once I could again see the church tower standing up like a stubby thumb over the thatched roofs. She did not say a word to me until we got to this point.

"See that other gray stone tower thing—nearer to us than the church—that used to be the village lockup. Not that anyone can remember anybody ever being locked up in it. We used to muck about in there when I went to school. Supposed to be the only bit left from an old priory. Monks all died in a plague. An archaeologist dug up the field round there and found a whole lot of graves. That was a few years back. The old boy who did the digging's dead now."

She had paused—was hesitating—almost as if she did not want to go in the village at all.

"You don't go to school here now?" I asked.

"Can't anymore," Chloe said shortly.

She led forward quickly, on up to the village street. I followed, imagining she must now go to some school in the county town. When she actually stepped onto the road, she paused again, looked left and right, and waited. It was a narrow little street that twisted round between the close-built cottages.

"This way?" I asked. I could not see that we could do anything else.

"Y-e-s. You will stay with me, won't you?"

"You're leading, I'll follow," I said.

Actually we walked together between the staring cottage windows that were all lace curtains and over flowing flower boxes. I saw a canary sunning in its cage outside one front door. Farther along an old woman was down on her knees scrubbing the step outside her door

I found that Chloe hung on to me as soon as we saw the old lady. I saw Chloe bite her lip and turn her head away and I wondered why. The woman scrubbed and we kept on. Only as we were just about to pass did she look up.

It was obvious, from the way her old face stared, that she knew exactly who we were. I shall always remember the look that moved across her face . . . a kind of sad surprise, as if we ought not to be there, as if it was a pity that we were there, as if it was a pity that *I* was there.

"God rest you, Chloe girl." Sideways glance at me. A shake of her head.

Chloe did not reply and neither did I and I felt uncomfortable. Chloe only hurried me on. She pointed ahead. The street was bringing us out into a little square.

"Used to have the village pump here . . . and the stocks. They've all gone, but there's something else still here. Look, Matt, up on the wall under there—high up—see it?"

I did see it, the second time I looked. I had to stand right back against one of the buildings and up on my toes at the same time. It was set in a little niche, high on a wall, almost under the gable of one of the old houses. It was a stone face, worn and weathered, but with the real expression somehow looking out from behind and through the battered stone itself. And although the stone was old, the face was young. I could not tell if it was a girl or a boy. The head looked one way while the eyes mischievously watched another, and the tongue poked out. But the tongue was not pushed out in derision. It was different from that. It was as if the tongue was tasting—tasting the world. And if the face was not laughing, it was surely about to break into laughter.

"Who is it—or what is it?" I asked.

"D'you mean Dock hasn't told you? That's the Brat of Elverley itself. Nobody knows whoever carved it or quite why they put it up there. But my mum can tell you all about the Brat and its part in the Elverley dance. Some say the Brat's the one who steals all the people's souls away—though in the dance it looks more like it's the Brat that gets stolen. Anyway, Dock sat here all one afternoon, on the top of a very tall ladder, drawing it. The constable got upset 'cause he said it blocked the traffic! Here, of all places! So Dock had to finish at five the next morning. C'mon, this way round."

"Well—give me a chance to look," I complained. She was so impatient. The face . . . you could so believe in it being able to steal one away.

We crossed over what was the main street, the one I had come down in the coach. I spotted the village shop. There was a bunch of village ladies gossiping outside.

"This way," Chloe insisted, going straight over, avoiding the ladies.

"Do you know," I said to her, "that Dockhurst has told the shop they mustn't sell me anything today? Not a pencil, a ballpoint, or anything—to make sure I won't draw!"

"Because he doesn't want you to draw?"

"I told you. He only wants me to look at everything."

"Oh, Dock can get our village to do anything —anything! They all think he's mad yet they all like him. He's awfully hard to say no to. Through the gap in the wall here!"

Unexpectedly, we were right over in the far corner of the churchyard. Chloe had paused. I was behind her. Her red hair swung left, right, as if to see who might be about, yet here there was nobody. I was seeing it for the first time in the light, seeing over the graves and between the trunks of the yew trees and up the paths that led to the gray stone walls. It was cool and peaceful here, the sunlight dotting through the branches and flickering on the tombstones. Some of them were overgrown, covered in moss and ferns, some fallen. Others, even some of the old ones, were well tended, had become sudden little gardens. We stood side by side on the path by an old seat where someone had dropped some marigolds; I gazed at a stone: SACRED TO THE MEMORY OF MARIA BUCKETT, DIED 1888.

"Gargoyles," Chloe was saying, pointing up at the church roof.

I had seen pictures of Elverley's gargoyles, had heard about them from my father. They were supposed to be unusual because they all had huge beards. They were carvings of old men's heads and torsos; leaning far out from the edge of the church roof, they were really there to shoot the rainwater clear of the stone walls. I stared up. The gargoyles all had their hands clasped behind their heads and half of them were smiling while the other half just scowled.

"But it's in the church you've got to see—what I want to show you—what Dock'll ask you all about. C'mon!"

I had wanted to stop and have a proper stare at those gargoyles—but she had got hold of my hand again. I had to follow.

With an easy familiarity Chloe swung back the wire-netted outer door to the porch. (The netting, she told me, was to keep out the birds.) Then she closed it carefully behind us before turning the massive black iron handle of the proper door. I can remember standing there, looking at the usual church notices: the appeal for the cathedral funds, the Elverley Midnight

Fête and Fair, the lists of the bell ringers. There was a place in the ancient wall that must once have held holy water. I saw that a marigold had been pushed in.

"Here we are," Chloe half whispered to me. The main door creaked.

It struck me as cold inside. I wondered how cold it must seem to Chloe with her bare feet on the flagstones, though she did not appear to notice. It was dim here—one could see the stained-glass windows full of blues and browns, a single beam of sunlight from a side chapel, the long and empty oaken pews. My sandals clacked over a grating.

"Over here," Chloe whispered. "It's right at the back. Dockhurst made it. I like to think it's the best thing in the church."

I followed her, wondering what it was going to be.

It was set in a hollow in the thickness of the old wall—yet it was quite new—carved in stone, a not-very-long stone box. Carved along its side in a high relief was a water rat running through rushes.

I opened my mouth—and then shut it again.

Piled beneath it, covering both the inscription and the date, was a mass of marigolds.

It was as if Dockhurst had brought the dead stone to life and had started it running. His water rat had wonderful feet and a tail; his rushes were growing.

"It's Dock who is really marvelous," Chloe whispered in my ear.

It was at this moment that I came to realize Chloe and I were not alone in the church. Sitting to one side and staring at us—and now rising to her feet—was the middle-aged woman with the streaky iron-gray hair.

It was from my face that Chloe realized that someone else was here . . . and looked round.

The woman herself was smiling at me in recognition, was coming forward to speak—while Chloe looked from the woman to me and back again, as if something had gone wrong, as if she could not think what we were going to say. Chloe looked as if she had been suddenly caught out, as if we were doing something wrong.

"Hello," Chloe broke in quickly, and in her full voice, not in a whisper at all, so that she made me jump.

Yet the woman took no notice of this, no notice at all. She took no notice of Chloe springing up toward her, but only of me.

"Hello, Matt—you have found your way here then. D'you know what you're looking at? D'you know who did it? It's nothing less than your friend Dockhurst's masterpiece. I think it is. *He* won't have any of it, mind you—about the work being any good. He will ask you all about the font carvings and the Tudor pulpit and those brasses over there."

"It's not his masterpiece," Chloe burst out. "It is good but it's not his masterpiece. It isn't even his sort of thing. You know it isn't. I know why you think it's a masterpiece."

The woman jerked her head, pulling her face away from where Chloe stood, her taut smile now vanished. I realized that she must be in some sort of pain. But it was as if the woman's own looking away was what hurt—not the looking at Chloe. Then she made herself look only at me, although I was of no importance.

"I'll take myself off and leave you to look round the church by yourself, in peace. I know Dock will want you to have a good look at it. See you later on, Matt."

She walked rather quickly down the aisle.

I stood there, just feeling terribly embarrassed. But Chloe ran round ahead of her, got to the big door first, unlatched it and pulled it open for her, held it so wide open that a flood of sunlight came pouring into the building.

The woman seemed nonplussed by this, uncertain what to do, whether to walk out into the porch . . . or for some reason of her own, to leave by a completely different door. And yet Chloe was holding the door open for her. They were hardly a yard from each other. Then I saw Chloe reach out a hand and just touch her sleeve.

"Good-bye," Chloe said, unexpectedly; although that was what she did say, she did not seem to mean good-bye. It was rather as if she were pleading for something, as if the woman would know just what she was pleading for. The woman swayed, as if Chloe's touch had been some sort of blow, and then without a word she brushed by Chloe and went out onto the porch. For an instant I saw Chloe watch her go, watch the woman open the outer door of netting beyond, fumble with the catch, open it, and shut it sharply behind her. Then, and suddenly I was thankful, Chloe swung her heavy door shut again and once more we were alone in the half-light of Elverley Church.

"Do you know who that was, Chloe?"

Chloe was pale, almost as if she were ill. She nodded.

"Oh yes," she said slowly. "I know who that is. I've—I've always known her. She . . . but hasn't Dock told you? No—he can't have told you then."

Chloe stopped. She was looking over my shoulder at the tomb that Dockhurst had carved for the church. For a moment I was afraid that she was going to cry. She pushed back the red hair from in front of her face. I found myself so wanting to say something that might help and found that I had no idea what to say.

"She—she never forgets the marigolds," Chloe went on, "even after all this time. I'm sorry this had to happen now. It was being a lovely morning. Let me—let me show you all the other things. Don't think I want to look at this just now."

So we didn't look at it anymore.

"You'd better go back to Dockhurst now," Chloe said. "It will be time for his snack. I know. It always is. I'd better leave you here. We might go up to the weir tomorrow. I'll try and see you first thing. You will try and come—won't you?"

"I'll come, Chloe," I promised. I wasn't quite sure how. I followed her out of the church. It seemed that there wasn't anything else that she thought I ought to see. I would have liked to have gone round more slowly, I would have liked to have gone back to Dockhurst's own carving, but I did not insist. Chloe closed the main door behind us, pushed me out into the sunshine, and then she closed the outer door.

"You won't tell Dockhurst too much, will you?" she asked me softly. "Not this time." And then, while I was wondering what I was not supposed to be telling Dockhurst, Chloe leaned over and kissed me.

"Don't you want to kiss me back?" she was asking.

I supposed that really I did. I stopped asking myself so many questions and just sort of kissed her back. She was awfully warm and then she laughed and with a wriggle she was out of my arms—and there she was running full pelt down the churchyard path. For a moment I stood still, not certain if I should follow her. And then I saw the rector, awkward on his bicycle, coming through the gateway . . . and it was obvious that he saw Chloe running toward him, because he swerved, Chloe swerved, the rector wobbled madly.

"Eeeeeh!" the rector screamed loudly. It seemed as though he swayed on that bicycle forever, and then there he was tumbling off and sprawling down among the gravestones. I found myself running toward him. It was only when I reached the rector that I realized Chloe wasn't anywhere.

The rector was getting onto his feet, a little shakily, and was rather ruefully dusting off his suit. I picked up his bicycle.

"Thank. . . thank you, Matt." It was a controlled voice. "A bit unintended, I am afraid. My imagination runs away with me sometimes. I suppose I wasn't looking where I was going. No—I am all right, I think. Just got back from Dock actually, left him getting your lunch. No, no, I will take the bike. . . ."

And he hobbled away.

5

You've had a good morning." Dockhurst told me through his kitchen window. "Lunch is all laid out in the garden," he shouted, having disappeared from sight. "What are you carrying your pajamas for?"

But he had gone so I did not have to answer.

It was not altogether my idea of a garden. It was really a sort of clearing where the grass had been trimmed down and the undergrowth hacked back from around a weeping willow tree. But there was a trestle table under it with benches on either side. The table itself had been well and truly laid. I counted five sorts of cheese on a board—not to mention a cream cheese with herbs in an earthenware bowl. There were three kinds of bread, too, and baskets of green-gages and pears, and, in the center, a mountain of green grapes. Sunlight spotted through the leaves and dappled all the tabletop. Under the tree it was like a tent.

I was wondering if I was supposed to sit down, or to go back and offer to help, or what, when Dockhurst appeared behind me with a jug of cider and two mugs and told me where to sit—but he had forgotten the butter, so I went and fetched it from his little scrubbed kitchen.

"Your dad always likes this stuff," he said, handing me a mug filled with cider. "Well—go on, boy—taste it!"

I remember it was a bit dry.

"You like it, boy, don't you? Of course you do. But never too much! Terribly bad for the liver, boy. I know—my liver's terrible. Hope you managed to do something this morning. Tell you what I did—a whole lot of nothing! Reverend Benn! He was here the whole morning. Marvelous! Great friend of mine. Always beg and pray I won't see him while I'm working. But it was no good today. His prayers were bigger than mine. Always do talk when Benn comes. Enjoyed myself, worse luck! Bread?"

I had bread. It was not very difficult to imagine Dockhurst talking the day through. I watched the way he was waving his arms about now. I wondered how the rector got a word in.

"It must have been him who passed me going," I suggested.

"It was. He mentioned he had seen you."

I thought I had better do some mentioning too.

"Saw him again on my way back—in the church-yard. He—he was falling off his bicycle."

Dockhurst stopped sawing at the bread.

"Falling off? That's not like Benn. Was he all right?"

"Oh, I think so. I did pick up his bike for him. That's how I know."

The bread knife went back into action.

"Good for you. Help yourself to that butter. See, boy, I expect you think old Benn's just the usual sort of dear old rector. Don't you believe what you see. The rector of Elverley's as hard as nails under that dog collar. Twenty years in the jungle he's been. Rumor has it that he was a cannibal witch doctor! So you did get to the churchyard then? Where else did you get to? Let me ask you my big test question. If you've been a failure you may as well know right from the start. Where can you see the Brat of Elverley?"

I did an imaginary jig all round Chloe. I could not get my answer out fast enough. Afterward, I swore, I would thank her two hundred times. I struggled to finish my huge mouthful of cheese.

"Isn't that what you see—it's a stone face high up on the wall—just round the corner from where the stocks used to be?"

"Bully for you!"

I watched Dockhurst being most satisfactorily impressed.

"Ha! And who told you about our stocks? Wasn't me. Must have been that rascal Benn. But did he have time? Not to fall off his bicycle *and* to tell you about the Brat of Elverley, surely? Perhaps you met Hester? Gray-haired woman talking about dancing on the green? Yes?"

I had cut off a bit of Dutch cheese. My father always calls it soapy stuff, especially when I'm eating it. I like it. I like it even more when nobody is telling me how soapy it is.

"I did meet someone like that. She didn't tell me who she was—though she knew you all right. Seemed to know who I was, too. And she said that she had found this barn for you."

I watched him listening to my reply, the dappled light all over him, his own face thoughtful and a little faraway.

"That would have been Hester," he said softly. "Owe you an explanation, really. Never told you before—but now that you are down here, you'll have to know."

He picked off what must have been half the bunch of grapes.

"Hester and I," he began very slowly and deliberately, almost as if he were rehearsing to himself rather than talking to me. "We are married, though we've been separated for some time. She . . . she won't come to the studio much these days, unless I'm ill or something."

Dockhurst looked up, seemed to have to look round to find me, seemed to want to see what I thought, rushed on before I could say anything.

"In fact I miss Hester more than I want to admit but I'm stupid enough to refuse to go back to the old cottage, much as I should like to. Yet she still—I mean she made all this bread and there is a chocolate cake because she knows you are staying here and so got old Benn to bring it over."

"Oh," I said. "I see," I said. I didn't see at all.

"Yet we—we don't live together anymore, even

though we like each other more than either of us cares to say. Something happened—perhaps it was because of me that it did happen. And I didn't behave too well afterward. A lot of it's been my fault. All a bit silly, if you want to know the truth of the matter."

"Oh!" I said again, rather uselessly, trying to get this sorted out in my mind and wondering what to say. "I'm sorry. But it wasn't . . . your wife . . . who told me about the Brat."

Dockhurst was dipping his grapes in his cider before eating them. It washed them, I suppose, but it seemed an odd idea to me.

"Who was it then, boy?" he wanted to know.

"Chloe," I said. "It was Chloe who took me all through the village. She was the one who told me about the stocks—and the Brat of Elverley."

Somewhere up behind us a wood pigeon cooed and called. I looked up—I then looked back toward Dockhurst. He was seated there with a big green grape about to be popped into his mouth. But it did not get there. He just sat, his elbows on the trestle table, and stared at me.

"Chloe?" he asked wonderingly. He seemed to be asking his garden more than me. "Chloe? You say you saw *Chloe* this morning?"

"Why yes . . . by the . . . you see . . . last night . . . she asked me if I would try and meet her."

Dockhurst took a long slow drink of cider. He stared at me across the rim of his mug. I wondered what was the matter. I was realizing that I must have given her away and I was kicking myself. But Dockhurst's question, when it came, was not quite what I had expected.

"Tell me, Matt—in the daylight—how did she

look to you? Was she . . . how was she? Well? . . . Happy?"

"She was great fun," I told him. I heard myself say it. Then an idea came into my head and I forgot to think before I spoke. "D'you know that when I saw her she was just like your picture? She was even down by the river and she was even wearing the same swimsuit."

It just slipped out. It took me two whole seconds to realize that it had come out.

Still he stared at me. Still he did not eat his grape. He did not even seem to have noticed what I'd just said.

"Did you . . . did you like her?" he asked me.

I nodded. I did like her, but why did he ask like that?

"And I like her, too, boy. Did she . . . did she ask you . . . did she ask you to swim?"

"Why yes, she did."

The grape was put down. He turned his face away from me. He would not look me in the face.

"Er—I didn't go in," I said lamely.

He groaned, and in a way it really frightened me. I had never heard a man groan seriously before.

"I am the idiot," he said. "Don't think I mind you swimming. And Chloe herself is a marvelous swimmer. But you see, you told me about her last night and I did not even have the sense to warn you. I said nothing. I'm thankful you're still all right. For you must not swim with Chloe. Any of the other village girls—but not Chloe. No—you could not possibly have realized why—or understood. I hoped—stupidly—that you would not have to."

I still did not understand.

"Hester—Mrs. Dockhurst—did warn me that the river might be dangerous," I began.

"It's not so much the river, boy," he said. "The river is obvious. It's not the river—it's Chloe herself."

He was looking at me and I can remember that it was torture for him to tell me, but I could see too that he had to tell me, just as I had to ask him.

"Chloe? What is the matter with Chloe?"

"The matter? The matter is I have known old Chloe for a very long time. Perhaps it is far too long. Matt . . . she is different . . . and I have to try and explain that difference to you."

A white cabbage butterfly flapped through the space above our table—over the loaves and the half-empty cider jug and the fruit. Outside the shade of our tree the sun glared down. Everywhere I could hear the zizz of the insects. I could feel all the heat. My clothes stuck to me a little. I could not grasp what Dockhurst was really trying to say. I could only feel his deep anxiety.

"Go over to the studio for me, boy. My picture of Chloe is still left out on the chair. Bring it back and we will look at it out here."

I found it easily enough. I was glad to be able to look at it, to stand there in the empty studio and look at it all by myself. It was marvelous how Dockhurst could paint her red hair as it was, flowing down her back. I could even see drops of water on the freckles of her shoulders. One of her shoulder straps had slipped, and she was twisting round. This was just how Chloe did stand. I could only stare at that canvas wishing that I, too, could make mere paints make her.

It seemed so normal, just staring at that picture. But Dockhurst had wanted me to carry it outside, had wanted me to make it normal no longer. Yet I did carry it out into his garden—carried it not wanting to take it—not wanting, suddenly, to know anything about it.

He managed to hang the picture on the tree. It was as if he had done this before. There was a nail. We both sat down again while he looked at his own work, looked at it so heavily it was as if he did not like it and yet would have liked to have liked it. I thought he was never going to speak.

Very deliberately, he began to peel a pear.

"Have you looked at the date?" he asked.

I looked at him. Then I looked at the canvas. There was a date there, tiny in the bottom right-hand corner, tinier than his tiny signature, but very clear.

It read eight years previously.

I stared at the face on the canvas, at Chloe looking back at me over her shoulder.

Eight years ago!

"Then—then this can't be Chloe," I stammered.

Chloe looked back at me from out of Dockhurst's canvas.

"I am afraid that this *is* Chloe," Dockhurst said gently. "We are sitting here together, Matt, here in the sunshine, and we are looking at my portrait of Chloe. I painted this all of eight full years ago. And you have seen her this morning. She has not grown up, has she? I have to tell you, I am sorry, but Chloe can never grow up . . . not now. She is always going to look . . . like this."

I went on staring at the canvas, staring as if my eyes could fight through and come out on the other side. I had to stare and stare at the canvas and only at the canvas.

"Who—who is Chloe, Dockhurst?"

"Our daughter, Matt. Hester's and mine."

I knew that he had put a piece of pear into his mouth. I could hear his heavy jaws chomping up and down. I had to wait for that chomping to stop. My mind was bursting with what he had said, with what Chloe had not said, with a terrible bewilderment, and a terrible understanding.

"But . . . she is well, isn't she?"

"Well—and not exactly well, Matt. You see, it was eight years ago that Chloe went swimming above the Elverley weir, went swimming all by herself. We had let her go a bit wild, Matt. Our fault. Though she was a powerful little swimmer. Hester and I weren't agreeing very much at the time. It was our friend Benn who found Chloe's body after it had been washed over the weir. Singlehandedly he managed to get her out. Then, still alone, he carried her nearly two miles to the nearest railway station . . . it was the only nearby place—and the trains still ran in those days. Little Oaken station—even then it didn't do much more than serve a quarry. Hester and I—they put on a special engine from Elverley to get us there. I shall never forget that ride. It was dark by that time. There was the flare from the firebox—we had to hang on to the swaying engine cab. They went as fast as they could. It would have been three times as far by road. The message was a bit garbled and we still hoped that she was alive. When we got there—they had put her in the waiting room, on the table. It was a cold little room. There wasn't anything that either of us could do. Nobody blamed us. We both knew that we were both to blame. Oddly enough, that was something we didn't disagree about at the time. I remember standing there with Hester, looking at Chloe, hating myself and feeling helpless. The others thought I was mad. You see, I started drawing Chloe, as she lay there. Drawing was all I knew, the only thing that came to me then. That was one thing Hester did understand about me. That drawing of Chloe's head I showed you last night? That was it. I did that eight years ago."

I seemed to hear his words without listening to them. Part of my mind refused to understand —another part understood only too well.

"But who have I been talking to?" My voice no longer sounded like my voice.

Dockhurst ate another piece of the pear. He did not speak to me at all. He spoke to his own fingers.

"Chloe's ghost."

Again I watched his jaws eat. And I knew that I believed him—even if I could not quite believe in my own belief.

"Before last night," he was saying, "Chloe really only came back to me, here. Oh—she's tried to appear to Hester, too—at our original cottage by the rectory—but Hester refuses to see her. My wife is rather commonsensical. She considers that seeing ghosts is a sort of weakness. I think she feels that the village would think her a bit dotty. The village does think that I'm a bit dotty, of course. But time after time Chloe does come back . . . and talks to me. Always she is as she has always been. She talks nineteen-to-the-dozen as she always did, about everything and anything—except as to why she comes back. Chloe only laughs when I ask her that. There are moments when I feel—almost that she is waiting for me to tell her why she has to come. She comes so often that I have long got used to her. Yet Hester still grieves terribly over our lost daughter . . . while in a curious way I have never lost her at all. If Chloe misses a few weeks then I am disappointed. But then she reappears again—she plays around the barn and chats to me, as she always has. I look forward to her coming. But so far—she has only really visited me. And now you, Matt, a comparative stranger, you have seen her in the full day, and last night when you arrived, then you saw her, too. Perhaps I have been a fool to talk to her about you and your visit. But I talk to her about everything I do. Last night I saw no point in saying who she was. But now it is you who have seen her in the middle of the morning—and you never even knew her!"

"The—the rector's seen her," I said. "That— that's why he fell off his bicycle!"

Dockhurst looked down at his fingers.

"Then she's showing herself to the whole village! D'you know, if she had still been alive, she would have been twenty-one by now. Hester will hardly be able to bear this—to know other people are seeing Chloe as she once was."

"But Chloe is real," I heard myself burst out. "She—she splashed water at me. I've held her hand!"

A glimmer of a smile crossed Dockhurst's face. "She is real, my boy. She is a very real ghost."

"But she's even pinched my pajama jacket. You

see—she came and saw me again last night—while I was getting ready to go to bed. And she ran off with it. I had to see her today to get it back. That's why I had it with me."

"Can't help that, Matt. She's been pinching my brushes, pencils, books, ever since she went. We play table tennis. She's nonetheless real for being dead —she's more! Yet in all these years she has never changed—she never grows any older. She is a ghost."

"But I've seen her swimming and she has come out and *dried*," I insisted, somehow certain that a ghost could not be wet.

"She even eats, Matt. Almost absentmindedly, a year after she was drowned, I offered her one of her favorite chocolates. She ate it! It disappeared! Then I found her turning up when I was having supper by myself and I would give her some. She didn't only enjoy it—she would forget to wipe her mouth and her face would be stained with raspberries. And yet, Matt . . . when we get to the winter, that's where it shows. I remember one of the first times I noticed . . . it had been snowing all day and it was still snowing. It was very late, and very cold . . . and all at once, in she came. She sat at my side, sat down on the rug, bare feet, bare legs, hair down her back. It had never struck me before—I put out my hand and felt her hair—it was sprinkled with snow. I tickled the back of her neck—Chloe always liked that. And then I realized that she was still wearing nothing under her jersey and that she ought to have been frozen. Yet she was still brown, she was six-months dead and she still felt as if she had just been running in the sun, she was so warm."

71

I remember Dockhurst sitting there at his trestle table, scratching the back of his head—and hardly talking to me, talking rather to himself. I thought of the old horse, that morning, and the dog, the night before; both had run away from Chloe and now I knew why. All at once I was feeling so very sad.

"Why—why do you think she keeps coming back?" I asked. Inside a part of me was also asking: come back from what? What keeps coming back?

"She doesn't tell me," Dockhurst said flatly. "She will not say anything about what happened, what happens, what she wants to happen, now that she is dead. She seems only to continue on and on as if she had never slid over the weir that afternoon, as if it all never happened at all. She does know that it isn't still eight years ago—but that's not something she ever wants to discuss."

It was at this moment that I made a discovery about myself. I had promised to see Chloe again. Somehow I knew that I must not tell Dockhurst what I had promised. And then it followed from that. . . . I realized it. . . . I was in no way changing my mind. Mad as it was I was still going to see Chloe. A whole side of me was not running away.

I watched Dockhurst's hands feeling their way around the table for grapes that were no longer there. His cider jug was empty, too. So he just went on talking, and his talk seemed so much more extraordinary than Chloe herself had ever been.

"And you see, boy—before she drowned—how I used to draw her. I was always drawing her—because she was always there. You've seen one or two things—but there are many, many more. Best model I ever had. She would put up with me for hours. Yet now that she is dead she won't sit for me, she won't let me paint her. I made a few attempts at first, but she stopped me altogether. I have asked her over and over again. Now she even gets into a kind of temper if I as much as look at any of my old things of her. That is why I hid this picture away—because Chloe can't bear it! I have to hide them all away. I can only bring them out . . . when I feel that she's not here."

He talked on and on. He kept talking until I reminded him that he was supposed to be teaching me— just to stop him. So we did do the washing-up together and he sat me down in the barn and at last we began. But all the time I could see that his heart was not in what he was doing, and that I was hardly listening either. It was not like Dockhurst at all.

He made me hide Chloe's picture away.

I did see another one of her on the rack—in it, she was eating an apple.

Dockhurst sent me out to draw. We were almost glad to escape from each other.

6

I did not go near the village. I did not go near the river. I did not go very far. I simply found and followed a small path that led me off the road and allowed me to be alone. It took me round the back of some old farm buildings and through the strong smell of pigs. Then it took me up the side of a field of turnips and through a hedge over a stile and then up again onto the open side of a hill. There was a stone wall there, and there I sat and sat, looking down at the view.

Again I could see the whole of Elverley, but the other way round and from farther away than I had viewed it that morning. Now I could see more of the green and what must have been part of old Bascombe's house and the roof of Dockhurst's barn. This time I was seeing it alone.

I could see it and yet I could not quite believe in it. Yesterday, at this time, I had been sitting in the coach. Now I sat up here. This morning I had talked to Chloe and it had been a somehow strange and yet marvelous morning. This afternoon I had been with Dockhurst and now that morning had become all bewildered. Now I was alone and Chloe had been made different. Dockhurst had at no time told me what to do and none of the things that I had seen, none of the things that he had told me, would quite join up in my head. So I tried to sit still.

I tried to tell my mind to stop turning over and over, to stop asking questions. I did try to make myself look round. Nobody seemed to be about. I got out my sketchbook, not certain that this was the right place to work—not just now.

Sunlight glinted on the distant river. I could see a line of long puffy white clouds sailing up from the south between the mounds. A jay flapped over a tree.

At least I was allowed a pencil this time. . . . Well—I hadn't been forbidden one!

I opened to a blank page in the sketchbook. Then I looked in front of me, considered what I saw, and finally I put a small upright mark on the paper, dead in the center. That was the church. It did not look like a church—but that was what it was. As soon as one makes a mark on an empty sheet of paper, then that sheet of paper has a place inside itself, an inner shape that it has never had before. You have begun and you can never go back on it.

I sat on my wall.

I looked up at the Elverley mounds on either side. How was I going to parcel them all out? I looked down at my paper.

And then I was hearing footsteps crunching on the cinder path. I did not look up. I refused to look up. I went on sitting and holding my pencil. My first thought was that I hoped whoever it was would not want to stop and talk. I had had enough of talking. I wanted Dockhurst's notice pinned to the back of his sweater: GO AWAY—CONFOUND YOU!

The footfalls seemed to come quickly up to me—and then to stop. I knew that whoever it was was standing close to me, was looking over my shoulder. So I had to look round.

It was the middle-aged woman with the iron-gray hair. It was Hester Dockhurst. She was standing there, waiting for me to notice.

I put down my pencil.

"Hello . . . Mrs. Dockhurst."

"Hello, Matt." She was smiling. She smiled with her eyes rather than her mouth. I could see all the countless little lines smiling at the corners of her eyes. "So you know now? Yes—I am Mrs. Dockhurst. I even enjoy being Mrs. Dockhurst still. There . . . there are only a few things that we really disagree about, Dock and I."

I didn't know, really, but I nodded and hoped that that was the right thing to do.

I was glad that she did not try and look at my sketchbook with its solitary mark. I certainly did not want to talk about that.

"It's his work," she said shortly. "My fault—I knew well enough what he was like before we ever got married. Everything always goes into his work. Anything else, anyone else, comes second. It was all right when I was his work. He used to paint me in those days. He was always painting me. I must have been the best model he has ever had. He sold everything he ever did of me. They were—our work. I liked being with him. He liked me being there. But I thought, when we got married, that we should have been able to do . . . just most things together. But with him his work was always just that bit more important. It was not that we didn't get on. He still thinks I'm marvelous. Likes me to be there. Always wants me to be with him, even if he doesn't say anything to me for hours and hours. But it is always his work that really has to come first."

"Yes," I said, listening to this outburst and wishing that it wasn't being aimed at me. But Mrs. Dockhurst hardly seemed to be noticing me at all.

"Then we had a daughter."

"Chloe," I prompted.

"So he has told you that?"

"Oh yes," I said, all at once afraid of what she might say.

"He's told you . . . ?"

"I've seen some of his pictures of Chloe," I said.

"Yes—he would show you those." She stopped. She started again. "He has never sold any of them. He doesn't need to. I wouldn't want him to."

"In the church," I began a little awkwardly. I had to say something. "Where you had put all the marigolds . . ."

"That's where Chloe lies," Hester Dockhurst said.

A breeze blew across my face. I managed to

shut my sketchbook. I didn't want it open now. Somehow I still wasn't being allowed to draw. I had come to Elverley to draw—to learn to draw, and Dockhurst did want me to draw—but now I was becoming part of the Dockhursts instead. *Chloe Dockhurst,* my mind said to me. I had not thought of that before.

"It was because of Chloe that you did not want me to swim," I said.

Hester was looking out over the same distance that I had been looking over. She was looking away from me.

"That's right, Matt dear. Chloe was always swimming. It was as if she escaped from us all once she was in the water."

There was a difficult pause.

"Matt—when I saw you . . . a little later this morning? When we were in the church? There was somebody else there, wasn't there? Apart from you and me? You were with someone, weren't you? I don't mean to be curious—but there was somebody there, wasn't there?"

I felt as if I had been caught in the wrong place with the wrong person. But surely Mrs. Dockhurst saw her, too? I was not sure what to say.

"I was with someone," I admitted. "I . . . I didn't understand why you did not speak to her. You—you must have known who I was with."

Hester Dockhurst was looking at me directly now.

"All these years, Matt . . . I have been seeing that hallucination—ever since Chloe drowned. I have seen her . . . in my garden, bouncing a ball . . . or she has come in and put down her books from school at half past four. I have walked into my own bathroom and she has left all her usual mess after washing her hair! And I have tried so hard not to see her. Yet now even strangers see my hallucinations. The whole of Elverley would have thought I was going mad if I had talked about it. *I* thought I was going mad. A silly middle-aged woman's delusion! I have watched Chloe come up and speak to me. I have forced and forced myself not to make any reply. I have walked into her old room on a Sunday morning and then seen her asleep, years after she had died. I have made myself walk out again. I have gone in later and seen her bed unmade—and I have refused to remake it. I always used to insist that she make her bed. Besides—how could her bed be there unmade? Yet later I would find it made. So I had imagined it, hadn't I? Dock kept telling me that he saw her. I blamed him for putting the whole idea into my head. I only wanted Chloe to be at peace. I didn't want her to keep coming back. Though I missed her—and I still miss her. I blame her, too. Chloe was always so independent. She was a very good swimmer and she should have had more sense than to have swum out above the weir. But Dock was always encouraging her to do things her own way. Perhaps that's why I haven't really been able to forgive him. And when Chloe was found—d'you know the rector found her?—we had to go to the Little Oaken railway station. That's where they laid her—on the table in the waiting room. She was dead, and Dock hardly spoke to me. All he could do was just stand there and draw her!"

I could only sit on the stone wall, going both hot and cold at once and only knowing that I liked Dockhurst and that it was a tremendous drawing and that I liked Chloe, too.

"And now you are seeing her, Matt. You are parading her even, up and down in front of her own mother. You must not see her. She is a madness and she is not real and she is not there!"

I opened my mouth and shut it again. Mrs. Dockhurst was almost shouting at me.

"Does she speak to you?"

"Why—yes, she speaks to me."

"She never speaks to me. I won't listen to her. Why should she speak to you? Does—has she told you why she comes back? I don't understand why Dock doesn't know. Why hasn't he told me?"

"He doesn't know," I said. "Chloe won't tell him."

"He imagines her," Hester declared, "but he won't imagine why she comes back."

"I don't think he imagines her," I ventured.

"We both wanted her to dance . . . for the midsummer Midnight Fair . . . for the Elverley dance. We both wanted her to dance the famous part, the Brat of Elverley. She danced so well. We were so proud of her. And do you know what that dance tells? Oh, it's a secret, Matt. It's a secret that is so painful to learn. That is why I shall tell it to you. It is different from what people think. For the Brat of Elverley is famed for stealing souls. The Brat steals souls from heaven and brings them into this miserable world. And that is death, Matt. And then the Brat herself is stolen— stolen back into heaven with all her ill-gotten gains. And that is yet another death—for those still living here. We knew that secret, Dock and I, when we wanted her to dance. We knew it . . . and we did not believe it. We thought of interesting old legends and literature and brilliant academics writing their oh-so-erudite papers up at Oxford. What a privilege to read about ourselves! What a privilege to live here! But it's the privilege of death, Matt. It is not the past in Elverley. It is not some old legend. We dance death here every year. Next year we shall be dancing death again. That is how Dock and I turned her into a thief, Matt. Don't you know that you are walking about with a ghost who is a thief and is herself stolen goods? Don't you know what you are doing—and what she may do to you?"

"I—I think I'm walking with Chloe."

"And Dock never even warned you, never even tried."

She was looking at me. There was pain across her face. I could not make out what she really thought.

"If Chloe tells you, Matt—if Chloe tells you why she comes back—you will come and tell me, won't you?"

"Of course I will, Mrs. Dockhurst."

All at once she turned very quickly—stopped—looked back at me.

"Thank you, Matt."

And then she started walking away with jerky little steps back down the hill.

I just went on sitting, my hand stroking the familiar hard cover of my own sketchbook, over and over again. I sat there a long time. I felt terribly sorry for her. But I knew I was terribly sorry for Dockhurst, too.

And for Chloe . . .

7

That night, when I at last got back to my room, I did not feel that I wanted to go to bed, and yet I was so tired. It was long past the time when I ought to have gone to bed.

Did Chloe have to sleep?

And I did not even know if Chloe *could* sleep. I only knew that I had to sleep. I had come up to this room to sleep.

Hadn't I already seen her in this room? The window was shut this time. The first thing I did on coming in was to see if it was shut. I remember looking out of that window and seeing . . . seeing nothing! It did occur to me that I had not seen a ladder anywhere—not one that would reach up this high.

This was the room where Chloe used to sleep. They were her mirrors that watched me getting ready for bed, that watched me look back at myself, that watched me put my comb through my hair, that saw me pulling off my shirt. Staring into her mirror over the dressing table I could see her mirror over her basin, her full-length mirror on her wardrobe door. Like me, Chloe must have looked at the reflection of the white sloping walls of this plain, high, wooden room built in the roof of Dockhurst's barn. I stared at it in the mirror over the basin. I watched myself wash. I saw myself undress and fold up my clothes. Chloe's wardrobe door creaked, clicked, shut awkwardly. I could see a reflection of three of my reflections shutting three mirrored wardrobe doors. How often must Chloe herself have padded round this room?

Chloe was not here.

The night was hot. I got straight into bed, covering myself with only a sheet. Apart from Dockhurst, I had not expected to meet anyone much on this holiday. My dad had never said anything to me about Dockhurst being married. And Dockhurst was supposed to be one of Dad's best friends. I had rather looked forward to coming down here and drawing with Dockhurst without being interrupted. . . .

I was lying on my back. I kept lifting my head off the pillow in order to look all round the room. In the mirrors, my reflected head came off the pillow and looked all round the room. None of Chloe's things were here. There were only my things. I could see my handkerchief, keys, knife, money, sandals on the floor.

This was Dockhurst's house. And today—today

had been the first time I had ever seen Dockhurst at a loss. Before, he had always been the great man, the artist other people talked about, the big confident man who had only to ask and everything was opened up to him because he was—Dockhurst! My mother used to say that he was a good friend not just because he could make the day seem so much more interesting—he could make you feel more interesting as well. He would always want to listen to you. He had been a marvelous pal to me. But today I had seen him being uncertain, having to untie all his secrets in front of me and trying to put up a good front, at a loss as to what he should do. But, didn't I like him all the more?

He was a giant-sized adult. Yet all at once I was having to share his life with him. Chloe was real. Hester was real. I could not understand what was happening, but because I was involved with them all and because I liked them all, it made everything better and worse at the same time.

I was lying on my pillow thinking and I at last became aware that I had not switched out the main light. I told myself that I would not switch it off just yet. Part of me was simply not sleepy. Would I be able to go to sleep? I could see the reflection of the light in the wardrobe mirror. . . .

I sat up. Everything was quite still. I lay down again. I think I must have gone off to sleep with the bedroom light full on and my eyes wide open.

Everything felt so different in the morning. When I actually awoke it was to find myself very comfortable. For some reason I had never expected to be comfortable. I was opening my eyes and shutting my eyes and staring at the early sunlight on the sloping ceiling. A dog barked somewhere in the far distance. I remembered having watched Dockhurst the night before, working on a painting of sunshine in his untidy garden. I had stood down there in the shadows of his studio, about to wish him a worried good-night, and had remained there for ages, spellbound, seeing him create his own sunlight.

Now I was staring up at real sunshine, but there was the main bedroom light still on. I should have slipped out, there and then, and switched it off before Dockhurst came up with the tea to wake me. But the bed was so very comfortable. Perhaps I closed my eyes.

I can remember opening them. A tap was running. Dockhurst had come! Perhaps—in all this sunshine—he would not even notice the light left on. Stealthily I turned my head on the pillow.

It was Chloe.

I was looking at her bending over the basin in the sun. It was such an ordinary thing to be doing. She was brushing her teeth and managing to send a spray of toothpaste up the mirror.

I watched her holding her red hair out of the basin with her left hand. The sun shone full on her bare back—I could see the curve of her spine with its knobbles—the movements of her shoulder blades as she was brushing. If anything alarmed me at all, it was the conviction that I was the one who should not have been there. It was as if it were me invading her, rather than the other way round. Did she even know that I was in the room?

I caught sight of her face reflected in the basin

mirror. Chloe was wiping her mouth. Our eyes met. She knew.

"You're using my towel," I exclaimed.

The face put out a tongue. It still had some toothpaste left round one end of its mouth. . . .

"Wondered when you'd wake up," Chloe said.

I was discovering that Chloe actually there made me afraid only of what Chloe might think. I was terrified of making a complete fool of myself.

"Thanks for the loan of your toothpaste," she was saying. "Never seen this make before. The new peppermint goo—with grit!"

I thought I'd better sit up.

"How long have you been here?" I asked.

"It's my room," she told me. It was not exactly an answer that said anything. She turned round. "You've got to get up as well," she added pointedly. "It's a long way. Sooner we're ready, sooner we eat breakfast, sooner we're gone."

And Chloe just went on standing there, combing out her red hair with my comb and waiting for me to move. I had no idea what to do. It seemed so much safer in bed. Out there she was in a different world. To get up and put one's feet on the fitted carpet beside her . . .

"But—" I began. It was as if I were afraid of her just because she was a girl.

"Dock won't mind us getting breakfast now. I often cook here. He won't wake up yet, anyway. He went on too late last night. I'll leave him a note. After all, he's always leaving me notes." She stopped in the middle of her combing. She was staring up over my head. "Hey—the light's on!"

I wasn't going to tell her. I got out of bed to change the subject as much as anything. I wasn't going to tell her that I'd left that light on because I was afraid of her.

Chloe fried up bacon and sausage and tomato while I was put to cutting bread, watching the toast, and making tea. Chloe buzzed round preparing a big picnic at the same time so that there was no doubt we were going a long way. I had to concentrate hard not to look inefficient—she was so deft and bossed me in loud whispers. "Now cut those sandwiches down the middle for me. No, use that knife, the clean one. And then you can wrap them up in the foil. Here, let me do it!" We were supposed to be doing all this ever so quietly so as not to wake Dockhurst, but I could not see how you could fry quietly. Chloe certainly couldn't. I felt better sitting down and eating breakfast. I knew what to do there.

Chloe stuffed down an enormous breakfast. I had to make more toast.

And we washed up afterward. I had to volunteer to wash because she knew where everything went. Then we left a big note propped up against Dockhurst's cornflake box: MATT AND ME OUT ALL DAY, LOVE CHLOE. I carried the picnic.

There was a hole in the hedge at the back of Dockhurst's garden. We went through that. The path beyond led both away from the road and from the village. I had no idea of the way . . . all was unfamiliar.

"You do still want to come with me, Matt?"

I had felt all right while we had been having breakfast. Eating breakfast was familiar.

"Of course I want to come."

Chloe did not seem to be half so troubled by the brambles and nettles as I was, and yet her feet were bare. She had on a different outfit today, a crisp blue cotton skirt and a white and newly laundered T-shirt with an anchor on the front.

"Matt?"

"Mmmmmm?"

"Now that you've stayed with him a bit, what d'you think of my dad?"

The path was narrow, overgrown. I was concentrating on following her heels. She had freckles right down to her heels. It took me a moment to grasp the importance of what she was asking. Did she know, then, that I knew? Surely she must realize that I now knew who she was. But did she? I had no way of being sure.

"Dockhurst?"

She made no response.

"Dockhurst is even more Dockhurst than I ever thought he could be. His studio's his world. He makes everything he sees and does belong to him. But you have to like it because he makes all the things you know seem bigger and better."

I could not see her face because she was walking in front of me. But it brought it home—that it really was her father we were discussing.

"That's just how he is, Matt. That's always been him. Have you noticed that everybody calls him Dockhurst? Or Dock, p'raps—if they know him well. Even I call him Dock. D'you know his Christian name? You don't—do you? It's Fred! Fred Dockhurst. But nobody ever calls him Fred. Never heard anyone do that, not even Mum. He's just Dockhurst. There isn't any other."

It was as if she wanted so to call her father Fred. Or so wanted somebody to call him that. She did not look back at me over her shoulder and I did not know what to answer. We walked on in silence. When the path widened a bit I managed to get back alongside her. As I did so she started talking again.

"It was for Dad that I danced the part of the Brat. Wouldn't have done it just for Mum. Dad seemed to understand what the Brat was really about even if he didn't know a thing about dance steps."

All at once I realized that although her head was turned away from me, her eyes were watching me— sideways. And as we looked at each other she deliberately began to make her tongue peep out between her lips—and it was as if that tongue turned to look at me.

It was only for an instant! I think that she realized at once what she was doing to me. The path in front of us was coming out into a field and she immediately seized the chance of changing the subject.

"Race you across!"

She was running almost before I realized. And I was the one carrying the basket. I pounded after her and I can remember thinking how she was really a bit younger than me—even if she had been born so much earlier. I sprinted and nearly caught up with her.

I think that was the moment when we both started laughing. She dodged sideways—I nearly stumbled; she doubled back—I followed. And then she was off at an angle and up a green bank. I swerved round after her. I could hear a touch of hysteria in my own laughter.

Ahead of me, high on the bank, Chloe was standing still. She had turned round and was waiting for me. She did not try to run. She was smiling. I found that I had been led up onto an old disused railway line. She stood so still.

There was no railway fence here. The track had once run above the level of the field—that was why there was a grass bank. The original lines had all been taken away and now there was only a simple path of cinders.

"Is this the disused Elverley line?" I asked.

Chloe first looked up and down the track. It was empty.

"I use it," she said. "This is the way I always come. It's mine. Even when the old trains ran— weren't many—there weren't ever other people up here. Now most of the village have forgotten that there ever was a railway. There's nobody now, 'cept me."

Not that there was much actually to see. Just an embankment with old cinders on the top. I could smell the scent of dry grass. A cuckoo kept calling above us in the trees beyond. But Chloe's voice was the only other human voice. It was curiously private standing there.

I too looked up and down the track. I had to admit to the fascination of it. It was like stepping up and over onto a very other place. This cinder track was sweeping in from some elsewhere, was going round toward a distant cutting, running on toward some different destination.

"Where does it come from . . . go to?" I asked.

I could see why I liked it. Yet it was a disturbing liking. Her railway skimmed just above the fields—it was as if the hill before us opened a little to let us through. Her railway seemed to be in the countryside, to belong to it, and yet to be of something else.

"It's supposed to come up from Spilcombe Junction and then through Elverley to here—then there's Little Oaken, Undermore, Swinbridge, and down to the other main line at Watermouth, if you look at a map."

The names did not mean too much to me.

"Which way do we go now?"

"Toward the cutting. Away from the village. This way."

"And it'll take us up to your weir?"

"Oh . . . almost. Be your weir, too. But there's lots of time before we need go there."

There was sufficient room for the two of us to walk along the track together, though Chloe walked rather to the side to avoid the cinders. There was no sign of the old rails. I did see a battered railway tie abandoned in the undergrowth and, later, a mysterious sign, close to the ground, which just had the number fourteen on it. Chloe took hold of my hand.

"Fourteen miles from the junction," she explained. "That's behind us. And we must be five miles from anyplace else."

I could not think up a good reason as to why I should not hold Chloe's hand.

We were entering the cutting. It was like being within high walls. You looked up and there were the trees climbing above you on either side; you looked ahead and the cutting curved so that you could not see where it was leading. A dark bevy of rooks called back and forth above us, black wings and harsh echoes. We were taken out of the sunshine into cool shadow and then carried back into the glare again. There, upon the bank ahead, I could see it, half-hidden by undergrowth and overshadowed by trees: we were being watched by a distant signal box.

I was wishing that the railway line were not quite so private. The cutting had closed round behind us. One could no longer look back at the open fields. Here, there were only Chloe and me. Chloe had hold of my hand.

I looked away.

"S'pose it's because you live in London," Chloe was saying.

Even her voice seemed out of place here. There was an oppressive feeling that one ought to whisper. And what was she talking about?

"I mean—you're not very brown, are you?" Chloe said.

"You only freckle," I retorted.

It made her let go of my hand.

"Don't—don't you like my freckles?"

"I like *your* freckles," I assured her. I did.

"I used to hate them—until one day I thought I might as well like them 'cause they're what I've got. People teased me about them and they're all over me. Have you seen the big ones?"

She stopped and pulled up her T-shirt and I had to stop and inspect a lot of midriff. I could see her breathing.

"They're so big yet they never join up. And it's not your fault not being brown if you live in London.

D'you know I never ever went to London? They were always going to take me but never got round to it. Never will now."

I answered without thinking.

"You should have come up and stayed with us, Chloe. We've got a spare room. You can even see the dome of St. Paul's from the window—if you stand on the end of the bed."

Impossibly, I was picturing myself showing her round my own room with my posters and the magazine cuttings pinned all around the walls. I was imagining everything being ordinary and the two of us going through the drawings in my portfolio and drinking coffee out of the big brown mugs we had at home. . . .

"Like to have gone to London," Chloe said wistfully. She pointed up at the signal box.

"Used to go up there, now and then. One of the signalmen was a friend of Dock's. Used to invite me up into the box sometimes and I'd share his tea. Always had apple jam. Let me work the signals, too— against railway regulations. Had to sit down whenever a train went by, so that nobody would see me."

Now that we were coming up to the signal box I could see that all the glass had long since fallen out of the big windows. The old wooden steps up the side were green and spotted with mold; some of the treads were actually missing and a bramble grew up through it all.

"Tell you—there's an old tap at the back that still works," Chloe said. "Show you and we can have a drink of water."

The basket was dumped down. There was a narrow path through the brambles at the side. I edged round after her. The path was well trodden but led simply to an old brass tap.

"I'm the only one who uses it now," she said.

Chloe had to use both hands to make it turn. When the tap did move no water came at all for a moment. And then it spurted so hard that she stepped back and trod on me. The tap gushed everywhere and she had to struggle to control it. I wished that there was more space on the path. It was hot, even hotter here, the insects buzzing in our ears, everything smelling of damp and rust and decay. I watched her crouch down and push back her hair, the face half-turned-up, the mouth drinking.

Why did she want to drink? Did she really drink? Why did she want me to come with her?

"Now you, Matt."

Her feet were wet, she had soaked her skirt, she was wiping her mouth with the back of her hand.

I knew I was shaking my head. All at once—and I knew there was no logic in it—I knew that I could not drink there. I did not want to drink where she had been.

"No—no thanks."

"But—you're hot, Matt. It—it's the only drinking place I have. I know we've got some drink in the basket, but . . ."

"I'm just not thirsty," I lied. I was certain that she knew that I was lying.

We backed out onto the track. Without a word I picked up the basket. We began to walk on through the cutting. I walked on one side of the cinders, she walked on the other.

"Matt."

"Yes."

"You—you don't like me now, do you?"

The cutting was even steeper and higher at this point; we were out of the sun and even the trees were disappearing.

Chloe came across the cinders. She hobbled on them a little and then she grabbed on to my hand. I wanted to throw her hand away. She would not let me. And her hand was as warm as mine and yet it could not be warm. It was an imitation of warmth.

"Tell me what's the matter, Matt."

I could not. I was not sure. I was not sure about myself, about her, about anything.

"You're afraid, aren't you, Matt?"

She spoke so softly. I told myself that if I did not look at her she would not be there.

"I can't blame you. I think you're being awfully good. I've so often been afraid of what's happened to me—over and over again—and now there can't even be any running away. I have to stay with what's happened."

"What do you mean? Why should I be afraid?" I snapped out at her and then knew that I was even more afraid of her actually answering, of her telling me herself.

She stopped on the path.

"Would you rather we turned back, Matt? We could stop anywhere here. We can't walk off the railway—but we could go back if you like. We could have the picnic in a field off the track. We don't have to go on. We can plan a different sort of day."

I had not expected that answer.

"Of course we're not going back," I insisted. It was me gripping her hand now, forcing us on. Perhaps it was me finding out that I, too, could not run away. It would have meant admitting that there was something to be frightened of, admitting it to myself. "We've come this far, haven't we?"

"But you may not like it, Matt." Chloe's voice wailed a little. She stood feet apart—jibbing. "I'm sorry, Matt. I seem to be doing everything all wrong."

Yet still I pulled her on. Chloe walked, awkward beside me and with a sort of glad stubborn unwillingness—and neither of us spoke. The cutting had begun to close right in, it had deepened further, it was going downhill. It had become black rock on either side with only mean ferns and rough grasses clinging to the ledges. There was only just room for our track between the cliffs. Chloe dragged her feet. I dragged my feet. Once Chloe stopped altogether and pushed back against me.

"Are you sure you want to go on, Matt?"

We went on.

We rounded another slow and shadowed curve. I can remember where a signal, the semaphore at stop and facing the other way, hung gaunt above our heads. At one place the rock had been hollowed out a bit beside the track.

"That's for the men who lay the ties," Chloe said. "So they can stand out of the way of a train."

I grunted.

Chloe kicked at the dust.

"Doesn't the line ever get clear of this cutting?"
I asked her.

Chloe did not reply. We walked on.

"Of course it comes out," she said at last.

I did not reply.

"You would come," she said, as if it was all my fault.

"But you must know how much farther," I said irritably.

"Yes, I do."

The sides of the cutting seemed to be leaning in. I had the distinct feeling that the next curve was going to plunge us round into a black tunnel.

8

But, in fact, the cutting fell away.
I pulled up short when I saw that. I even let
go of Chloe. She stood away from me, just watching. She had been quite right. I did not want to go on.
Yet not for any of the reasons I had expected.

There, not three hundred yards ahead, our track
was leading out over a sunlit, sparkling, flowery, open
meadowland. Somewhere a lark was singing, singing
and spiraling down toward us. The air seemed fresher,
emptier.

It was as if Chloe were waiting for me to make
up my mind.

Out here, here on the other side of the hill, the
land was not farmed and yet it hardly seemed to be
wild. Perhaps it was used by sheep, though I could not

see any. There were flowers everywhere—yet they seemed so small. We had come out into a new place. But somehow it only made me more afraid.

I could still see where the rail track went on, where it bent away, running up the valley, up toward distant trees and a high cliff gouged out of the farther slopes. The whole meadow was a cloth of colors, of countless greens and pinks and yellows, with deliberate red outcrops of rock and shale spilling out among the flowers.

I tried to look away from Chloe.

The track might have led up through a careful garden. The whole meadow looked kept and cared for and yet so endlessly empty. There was this extraordinary sense that there could be no one here but our two selves. Everywhere the meadow bloomed in a somehow marvelous fashion, yet this only gave me an uneasy certainty that I was simply trespassing. It was as if Chloe ought never to have brought me. It was as if I should not be seen in this place with Chloe. . . . And yet there was no one here to see us.

"Will you still come with me?" I heard Chloe ask.

I looked down. I could avoid seeing her by looking down. But even then I had to look at countless tiny blue flowers, at a silver butterfly skimming above their heads. I did not reply.

Chloe moved nearer. I could just see her feet.

"Look behind you, Matt." She was pointing back the way we had come. I had to look.

It was toward the cutting. I knew my way back from there—yet now I could no longer see where we had come from. But what Chloe pointed to was a battered board by the track, reading in the other direction.

WHISTLE, it said.

And as I looked at it, Chloe whistled.

I jumped where I stood.

Chloe's whistle was a long, riveting, piercing, warbling scream. She let go more of a shriek than a whistle.

"When I was small," Chloe said behind me, "we used to go on the train along here. Sometimes I imagine it coming along here still. It was only a little train —on the one track. Whenever I walk along here, especially when it's dark, I think I can hear it steaming up behind me through the cutting. It used to really struggle up the gradient back there."

For a moment I had to picture it: the clouds of smoke and steam, the glow from the firebox. . . . The image became vivid and I had to ask, "How many years is it since they closed the railway?"

Chloe turned her face away at that—I knew that I should not have asked it, that it was unfair to have asked her. Yet she smiled at me afterward, though she did not answer. For an instant I stared at the sun on her hair—then she spun an exuberant cartwheel away from me so that she would not have to answer. I could only watch her legs swing over, watch her come up on her feet as easily as she had gone down on her hands, and then she was running away over into her different world, over the greensward and the blue flowers toward the high overhanging trees. My mouth and nose were filled with the sweet clinging scent of honeysuckle. Chloe was looking back at me, feet apart, hair comically across her face. I knew I could only follow.

I told myself over and over again that I knew that she liked fried tomatoes, that her father's name was

Fred, that she wore briefs that had blue polka dots on them. These were ordinary things. I was even glad when she took hold of my hand because I was becoming afraid of myself. I had found myself wanting to run away from her and toward her at one and the same time.

The track at last leaned round to the right—unexpectedly—after we seemed to have been walking endlessly over meadows, and there, all at once, nestling under tall and gently waving trees, very alone and secret, was a railway station.

I did not have to be told where I was.

"Little Oaken," Chloe confirmed. "Nothing here now. Not really a place at all. Used to be a village and a quarry. When they closed the quarry the village went, too."

"Is—is that why they closed the line?"

"Didn't help. There was an awful row when they shut down the quarry. My mum was one of the protesters, not that we ever lived here. She organized a meeting in Dad's studio, much to his surprise. And everybody ended up shouting."

In spite of the fact the railway lines had vanished, it was so obviously a railway station. There was this huge sense of arriving in spite of the empty and overgrown appearance. Here was another signal gantry, this time without its signal, and there a porter's trolley without one wheel, lying where it had been left on a weed-covered heap of ballast. . . . I found myself almost tiptoeing up the platform ramp where the grass and moss and dandelions now grew up between the stones.

Chloe had let me go on ahead.

Under the overhanging platform canopy were only blind and empty windows. I stopped to read the nameboard, a bit of it missing, rather rickety: ITTLE O KE . The doors, unlike the windows, had originally been nailed up and now the nailing-up had mostly fallen down. There were doorways for LUGGAGE, GENTLEMEN, WAITING ROOM, and a WAY OUT that led into a nettle bed. A smaller sign still asked one to SHEW YOUR TICKETS PLEASE. I wondered why they had spelled it "shew." There was a shattered oil lamp on a windowsill.

"If you're thinking of going in that Gents," Chloe called out to me, "—don't!"

"Why's that?" I asked, somewhat absently.

"Floor gives way. You'd fall through. It's all rotten in there."

"How do you know?"

" 'Cause I almost broke a leg. Would have been awful. There's almost no one ever about. Dock won't ever come here now. Don't think he would even think of looking for me at this place—'specially in there. Would teach me to be curious. 'Course they haven't even *got* a Ladies."

I stopped to look at the waiting room. It was long and narrow, dank and shadowed. Water had got in at the other end and stained the wall. There was a fungus growing over what must once have been a poster and the colors had streaked, faded, and now bubbled. The floor was thick with dirt and leaves. Yet, in the center, splattered with the droppings of birds, in this otherwise empty room, there was still the waiting-room table.

"Chloe," I said.

There wasn't any reply.

When I turned round I saw, by itself, in the middle of the platform, our picnic basket. A bunch of rooks went flapping by high overhead, cawing lazily to each other across the sky.

I looked up and down the platform. Chloe wasn't with me. Everything was empty, everywhere. There was only this basket on the platform, only last year's leaves, only the broken glass. The railway had stopped, the lines had all been taken up, the weeds and brambles had moved in. The edge of the platform was crumbling away.

Chloe wasn't here.

I found myself running up the platform. I remember running back, stopping, looking all ways. I went from LUGGAGE to GENTLEMEN to WAY OUT. But the WAY OUT was to nowhere, the GENTLEMEN had rotted away, there was no place for LUGGAGE anymore. There was only our basket with its picnic lunch.

My heart was thumping against my ribs. I found I was telling myself that of course Chloe could not be here, that she could never have been here, that I alone must have brought the picnic basket.

Yet it was just then that I did catch sight of Chloe. She was all by herself on the other side of the track, out on the meadow, practicing her slow cartwheels. She was going up sideways, staying up there, pointing her toes . . . and then coming very slowly down the other side.

She did them beautifully, unfolding herself like a fan, so that upside down her hair poured golden from her inside-out skirt down into the grass, her bare legs stretched Y-high up above her in the sun. Then, with perfect mastery, she folded herself up again, tossing back her hair as her feet returned together on the ground. And then I watched her slowly turning back, unfolding round the other way.

Chloe was still with me.

I found myself snatching up our basket, jumping —almost falling—off the deserted railway platform, running back across the track toward her with a desperate relief.

9

I'm starving," Chloe announced.

Eagerly, I suggested that we should eat. Where we were would do. I would set it out. She seemed to like the idea of me getting it.

Chloe said: "We could picnic on the platform —under the shade of the canopy."

Chloe let me sit her down on the edge of the platform while I set the picnic out all round her. I could not help but be amused, while I burrowed into the basket, at all the bits and pieces we had brought with us. No wonder it had been so heavy. It was obvious that she had been rather looking forward to us having all this. And it was not so much the food, which was ordinary enough as I remember—our fresh-cut sandwiches and the plain apples and bananas and Coke—it was the extras. I spread out the white cloth between us on the platform. There were two plastic glasses. There were two white paper serviettes. Chloe wanted it sort of formal. Not that I asked her at the time. I simply cottoned on. Looking back, I know it was exactly the right thing. Behind us were the still staring waiting-room windows, the shattered oil lamp surrounded by its scattered glass, the doorless doorways looking down. But I could open the Cokes and pour Chloe her drink. I could pass it across. She smiled as she accepted it from me.

"I'm famished," Chloe said.

I sat there, watching her. Her red hair had fallen across her face. She was eating what was really one of my sandwiches (only I hadn't told her). For the first time she paused, mouth somewhat full, knees drawn up, feet on the cloth, her skirt full of crumbs.

"You're not talking again," Chloe said.

I grinned at that.

I still could not see her face properly. She had put her head a little on one side—as if she were waiting for a real reply from me.

All at once I got up and, carrying my plastic glass, I walked round the cloth and deliberately sat tight down beside her.

And then we both didn't speak. It was as if we were each waiting for the other one. At last I said it. "Chloe—thank you for bringing me even this far."

Her green eyes stared at me.

"It's been a marvelous morning," she suggested. She in no sense moved away.

"No, it's not that, Chloe. It's because you realize I know who you are and yet you've still brought me along."

She had not quite expected that. For an infinitesimal moment her gaze shifted and then returned.

"Do you really know who I am, Matt?"

"I think so. But you tell me then. Say it out loud. I'd like you to tell me."

She seemed to be considering my request.

"You know that I'm Chloe," she said very simply.

Her face was terribly close. I was staring at a fascinating little pockmark set among the freckles between her eyebrows. I could see the minute down over the surface of her forehead.

"But I *really* know," I told her. "I *know* you're Chloe Dockhurst. You're the one they remember because she happened to get herself drowned in the river. You're Dock's daughter, the one who's dead. That's what they say. But you won't say."

She seemed to think about it. Ever so slightly, she swayed.

"They—that's what they've told you?" she asked.

I nodded. With a rush I was declaring myself to be on her side. Though it was almost as if . . . she was not going to accept what I had said. Yet she did not in any way deny it. Only—only it seemed as if I had to wait forever for her answer.

"Well?" Chloe said. And she sounded so curious. "And what do you think?"

I reached up and took a strand of her red hair between my fingers. Now she did not move her head. I even ran my fingertips along her eyebrow and over that pockmark and down that nose. She let me—but she did not smile.

"They—they have told me that you're dead,

Chloe. But you're not dead to me, are you? Are you? How can you be?"

She pushed my hand away from her face, but reluctantly, almost as if only to protect me.

"I—I am what you'd call dead, Matt. It's what I call—well, being 'otherwise.' All I want is for you to talk about it with me. I want you to say what I am—find out what I'm like. All I want to do is to share it a little. And I promise I won't turn into something horrible or anything. It's not like having a disease. I'm much the same as I always was. Don't know what else to be—yet! Becoming otherwise happens to everybody."

Yet she shuddered a little and she looked away from me.

"But Chloe—I can hear you. I can see you."

."Don't you like seeing me?"

"Y-yes. But if you're . . . dead . . . I'm not supposed to see you."

She picked up an apple. It was something to do. Yet I could see clearly that she understood.

"You can bend rules sometimes . . . sometimes it becomes possible to see the otherwise. Shouldn't often happen. Usually, there's no need—we don't want to be seen."

There was a hesitation in Chloe's voice as she told me—and yet an excitement as well, that she should be doing it at all. Perhaps I should not have listened. Perhaps we should have had no discussion. Yet between us, how could we have avoided . . . what she was?

"Chloe—why do *I* see you?"

"Starts with lots of reasons. Don't understand all

of them. One is—I don't want to go on because I think my leaving was my fault. And another is because Dock and Mum won't send me on—because they think it was all their fault. And at the same time they're afraid of me. Underneath I scare them—even Dock; I scare the whole village. I never wanted to frighten. I don't blame them, not really. I know it's to protect themselves that they refuse to believe in me. It's as if they never wanted me to be born. They only want to think of me as nothing."

I watched her as she crunched the apple. She looked so pale. I took hold of a strand of her hair and, very gently so as not to hurt, I pulled at it so that she had to move her head a little.

"You don't seem to me like a nothing, Chloe."

Again she put my hand away—but not in the least bit crossly. Rather, it was as if, now that I really knew, it gave me a chance not to touch her, as if I might not want to touch her.

"Matt, my mum even—when she sees me—she won't look, even when I'm standing right in front of her. You've seen her do it. She won't admit that I'm here 'cause I'm supposed to be a nothing! She only wants to remember her own memories. Yet I am as I was. And 'cause I'm not supposed to be here, everybody hates seeing me. They all insist I'm not here—except Dock . . . and now you. And Dock only sees me 'cause he refuses to admit that anything's ever different. And he doesn't really want me different. He wants to persuade himself that I never really died. But I'm so tired of staying still. They none of them see me as learning and changing and wanting to go on. They none of them see me properly at all. It leaves me so lonely. And I know they still really love me . . . yet somehow they can only hurt me. My mum loves me! And I love them. But I have to go on hurting back! It just goes on and on and there never seems to be any way out."

I could understand that. Already, this morning, I had been hurt, and she had not meant it.

"But Chloe—you still don't explain. I could never have known you before . . . yet I see you."

The apple core was thrown down on the track.

"Wondered if you would. When I waited for your coach—thought you might not see me, 'cause to you I really would be a nothing. Even if you did see me, I thought, you might not have come with me. It was wonderful when you talked, when you walked back with me to the barn. I had only come out on the spur of the moment when I guessed Dock had forgotten. Think it worked 'cause you knew my father so well, sort of knew him a bit like I did. And you didn't know anything about me so you couldn't be scared at first. Found that out from Dock. Asked him if he had ever told you about me. He'd sort of wanted me to stay away. We had a row almost. That made my mind up. Then I got so afraid he'd stop you coming. I just wanted an ordinary friend."

I can remember her saying that so earnestly . . . and I can remember at the same time so wishing that we could be ordinary.

"Do you—are you forced to go back to the weir then, over and over again? Is that what you have to do?"

Again Chloe waited—as if she were not sure how she could tell me—uncertain as to whether I would understand.

"In a way, Matt, I do have to. But also—it's my performance, the only one I've got. It's all people ever know about me now—me going back to the weir. Used to be a happy place, really—even if, ever since I can remember, Mum was always warning me about it whenever we went. But we used to enjoy it. When I was small, she used to hold my hand. There's this narrow bridge across it and we used to stand there for ages looking at the water rushing and roaring away beneath our feet. I used to be bewitched just watching all the white foam going over its edge. We could never hear each other speak. Yet the water behind us, just before it went over, always looked so smooth and still. There was a place on the other side where I liked to play. It was out of the wind. Sometimes Dad would find little harvest mice for me. He was good at those things. Sometimes he used to draw me. Mum and Dad agreed in those days and we really went up to the weir 'cause that was where he most liked to paint. We would often go out whole days for his painting. Never knew then what was going to happen there. I remember Mum trying awfully hard to stop Dad boring me by making me sit too long, when really she *had* taught me how to do it and I really *did* like sitting for him. It was always Mum who told me how good and patient I had been. Dad never bothered. It was Mum who always rewarded me with a piece of fudge at the end— but it was as if Dad got all the credit for it. Just as it was Mum who taught me to swim so well—because *she* can. If I was good at math at school, it was because Mum taught me how interesting it could be. But when I got the prize it was Dad I wanted to tell first."

"Your mum," I blurted out, "she told me that Dockhurst won't go near the weir now."

Chloe winced.

"That was after I went . . . after I drowned. He changed completely and yet he still wants to pretend that nothing really happened. Mum has tried to get him to go back, but he won't. Yet in the old days he was always painting there. If it wasn't me, he would paint Mum. When Dad took us off to lonely places, I didn't mind. It was when he wanted to paint me playing on the beach at Watermouth or somewhere that I hated it. People would crowd round to watch. At the weir, though, there wouldn't be anyone else, 'cept Dad and Mum. I've always liked going there."

I reflected that this was where we were now going to go. I remembered that I was to be her ordinary friend. We had moved a little away from each other now—and the odd thing was that this did not matter anymore. In some fashion we had both discovered that we could bear each other, at least for the moment. However dangerous our conversation might become, we could continue this talking. I was only afraid of stopping talking.

"Chloe, did you like sitting for your father?"

"Not as much as Mum did. She always felt she was doing something wonderful. So she was, for Dock. She was always telling me, teaching me, how I was helping Dad. I didn't mind that much—p'raps sometimes I did—but it was fun to see what he made of me. Used to earn a Mars Bar. And extra pocket money. And I always told him what I thought he'd done. Mum used to call me out sometimes but Dad did listen."

"Do you know, Chloe, they never told me why you went over the weir, the very first time."

For a moment she stared down at the track beneath our feet as if wondering how to answer.

"Surely . . . surely they told you that I went over the Elverley weir eight years ago 'cause I would swim where Mum told me not to! If they did, they were right. They told each other that I went over 'cause they weren't with me enough. P'raps they were right again. Now . . . the only thing that's supposed to be left is my new tomb in the church. I wanted you to see it 'cause it's Dad's design. Village didn't like it too much 'cause it reminded everyone of what had happened. It's as if people don't want to remember too much of what really does happen—but Dock *would* do it like that, and they couldn't stop him. I like it. Yet, you see, even though Dad made my tomb, he still won't face the fact that I've gone."

She stopped talking then. I could hear the cuckoo, somewhere far behind us, somehow adding to the silence. My answer seemed so obvious, yet so cruel.

"But you haven't gone," I told her softly. "You keep coming back."

"They won't let me go," Chloe protested in a small indignant voice.

"You don't leave them," I continued. "You come back."

"Do—d'you want me to go, then?" Her face was almost angry.

"No. But I think you want to go."

The silence hung endlessly—on the warmth of the air. At long last Chloe looked round at me, gave a dumb nod.

"I just come back. I'm drawn back. You're right, Matt. I'm on a horrible sort of roundabout. It goes on and on and I go forward and back and can't change."

"Chloe—where do you come back from?"

It was as if she had been stung. She drew away in sudden panic.

"Matt, you mustn't ever ask me that. It's too dangerous for you to know. You mustn't ever."

"Why?"

"You mustn't even try to know."

I can remember being surprised that I had so jolted her. But not only surprised. I became curious. And not only curious but somehow betrayed. She had been showing me her secret, sharing it with me, and now she wanted to stop short. We were trusting each other and now she did not want to trust me any further.

"Wouldn't I understand better if you tried to tell me?"

"It's too dangerous! Dangerous for you, Matt. Bad enough you being with me like this. You mustn't know where I go to. If I were to tell I might damage you, as I damage everyone else I know. It's a question that ought to be forgotten—for your sake, Matt."

The great meadow stretched away from our railway station, away and up as far as the eye could see toward the Elverley mounds. I sipped the remains of my Coke. Neither of us spoke.

At last I said: "I'm sorry, Chloe."

We met each other's gaze. Yet Chloe looked away from me, almost at once.

"I'm sorry, too, Matt."

But then the green eyes looked at me again—and I was startled to see how full of pain they were.

"Matt . . . if I said . . . if I told you . . . where I go . . . you would only learn to hate me. And I'd hate myself for doing it. Just as I hate myself every time I find myself coming back. They tell me I can choose and yet I find myself returning over and over again. I come back. You should never have been told that I still go on. Just a guess—that you don't quite believe in—that's all you should have had. That would have been safe. But, Matt, you know far too much already. You won't ever be able to stop asking questions. That's how I've betrayed you. You'll even hate me if I tell you that nobody would stay back here in your world, if only they knew. Your world's only funny shadows. When you're otherwise, then everything's more real than here. D'you understand, Matt—it's *you* who are the ghosts. You're the cold ones. You're only specters—just shadows waiting to begin. Only—you mustn't ever begin until you're ready. That's what's happened to me. I wasn't ready. . . . I still can't get all of me to go on. Part of me stays here. That's what's so awful—I *am* otherwise but I can't *stay* otherwise."

All at once she was on her feet, had pulled away from me. She was walking down the deserted platform and I could hear her crying. Chloe was sobbing her heart out in the doorway where once the luggage went.

Everything else was so still. The sun beat down beyond the station canopy. Even the cuckoo was silent. I could see a trail of ants already marching on our tablecloth.

10

Together—well, at least Chloe *tried* to help—we packed up the picnic. And we did not say too much. It was obvious that we were going on. We had to walk to the weir. But that was one thing we had not bothered to explain to each other. I felt that it had not been the thing to ask. Chloe knew that she had said too much already. Chloe was brave. To her, I think it was a relief to help me pack the basket. To me, I was glad to stand once more in the sun.

"Come on, Chloe," I said. "Shake the cloth with me. Want to get the crumbs out of it."

She picked up the other end. We could both see the expressions on each other's face. We both knew that it wasn't crumbs we were thinking about.

"Only—only have to talk to me, Matt," Chloe said in a rush. "Or not talk to me, if that's how you happen to feel. Do walk with me, even if you do know what I am. Please don't go away."

We shook the cloth together. We nodded in agreement at each other. Chloe did remind me that the cloth should be the last thing to go back in the basket. And she wanted to make quite sure that we had forgotten nothing. It was at her suggestion that we buried the Coke cans instead of taking them with us. And so I dug them down into the heap of ballast. Then she had wanted to do her nails and I had lent her the nail file on my knife. I offered her my comb again, too, jokingly asking her whom she thought we were going to see.

"You're going to see me," Chloe pointed out.

When I got my comb back we wrangled over which of us would carry the picnic basket. She won— she carried it.

The railway track led on and up. We passed a stack of old railway ties left rotting in the bracken. At one place I even spotted lumps of coal, once spilled by some steam locomotive and now long embedded in the soil. There was still a sign—19—nineteen miles from the junction. The green meadow was narrowing, the line curved round into a silent forest of pines. A tree trunk lay across our track and pine needles cushioned our feet. It was a long walk through muted gray shadow and under black branches. It was somehow solemn in there and we did not talk much (Chloe did not seem to mind), and I noticed the birds did not sing there either. Only once was there an opening where the sunshine cascaded through, and then Chloe simply pointed upward and I looked and there was a farther towering mound across the valley. After that we were back within the forest, with its gray gloom and continual silence.

"Chloe?" I asked in an undertone.

"Yes," she whispered back.

"Why did you go over the weir—the first time?"

"All so stupid. Started with Dad wanting to do this special picture and use me as his model and Mum wanting me to dance so that she could show me off at the Elverley Fair. They sort of forgot that I wanted to visit London, that I was trying to collect moths, that I was doing competition swimming down at Watermouth. S'pose I was selfish. But Dad's world was all his own in his work and Mum shared her life between Dad and the village. Apart from him, she was always doing things for the community, never for a person. Village isn't everyone. Village isn't anyone. I discovered that. Village was really something in Mum's head. But I wanted to be something in Mum's head, too. And outside it. Now Mum thinks a ghost is a sort of disgrace to the village. Prefers to pick marigolds and just stick them round my new tomb!"

"But Chloe, why did you go over the weir?" I persisted.

"It was an accident, Matt! It was a stupid accident and it was all my fault—not anybody else's. But I had swum the weir before. Of course I'd been told not to. Not only by Mum. Everybody said not to. Right they were. But I had done it three or four times already. You have to swim hard, but if you do, it doesn't take you down. You do get across. Did it! Had to try it when no one else was there, though. Couldn't ever get

118

the boys to swim there. But I swam. One time I even did it in the dark. Just to prove I could. Took my things off this side, walked across the narrow bridge to the other side, swam back. D'you know it was standing there on the bridge, watching the water foaming and falling over and down under my feet that made it so scary. Wasn't anyone about, of course. Just a few sheep. Wind was a bit cold. The bridge only had one rail—to hold on to. But I made myself stop and look, and then look again. Made myself walk on over and then swim back. Wasn't any sun to sit in after, either."

I stared at her with a kind of appalled admiration.

"But Chloe, why did you have to do it?"

"Just for—just—'cause I had to do it! I don't know why."

"So—if you could swim it—what made you go over?"

We walked. . . . We walked for some distance before Chloe replied.

"It wasn't night that last time. Lovely afternoon, really. And I was angry. Mum wanted me to go with her to this do at Lower Spilcombe. Lady Somebody was going to open their flower show and we were going to do the folk dancing. Mum was in the middle of all the arrangements, as usual, even though it wasn't our village. Mum always is. She wanted me to wear an awful new dress I didn't like, and it was the wrong length, and we had a row. And I'd sat for Dad in the morning and he had hardly talked to me and had got angry with his own work, which was hardly my fault. So I walked out on Mum and refused to go. Mum had to go. I was steaming cross and I walked and walked to the weir. The weir was a favorite, private place. I was going to swim just to annoy Mum—even if it wouldn't really annoy her because she wouldn't know! She was annoyed enough anyway. Or I'd tell her! Yes, I'd tell her what I did, during the flower show. Then I undressed. As soon as I'd done it I had this silly impulse to put it all on again—everything, even the shoes—and swim across like a lady. I'd lady 'em! And it would spoil the dress—DRY CLEAN ONLY! Remember reading the label. Must have been mad. Yet somehow, it was exciting going into the water all dressed up. I knew I was a good swimmer, and it wasn't until I got to the middle that I found that I couldn't swim quite so well, not with all that on. It took me some time to realize that I wasn't going to be able to swim faster than the current, that it was taking me and that there was no escaping. I remember that I didn't even panic. All seemed so inevitable. I had made a mistake. Found myself deliberately taking what I thought was to be my last look at the sunshine while I was being banged from side to side. . . ."

I could not reply. I hung on to the fact that she could not, would not, tell me any more; that that was the end, that there wasn't anything else to say.

"It was funny—there wasn't any pain. Only a long, long time when I knew I knew nothing. It seemed like days when I only knew a sort of ringing blankness. And then . . . when I saw again . . . I did not understand anything. Only that nothing hurt. I never felt anything. Only, I knew that I ought to have been in agony and I felt so perfect—and it was wrong. It was like being free and there being no point in having any freedom. . . ." Her voice trailed away. For some steps she walked on in silence. "But then I'm not supposed to talk about that," she whispered.

"We're not going to talk about it," I assured her.

"I'm only coming to the weir because it's a marvelous place to see, because your father liked to do a lot of his work there. If that's what you want."

Chloe glanced gratefully across at me.

"Just want you to come with me," she said.

The pine needles lay thick where the railway once had been.

At length the track ahead began to come clear of the forest, the trees started to thin out, the sunlight began to come through. The railway was coming out high on the side of a new valley. I touched her on the arm.

"Wait for me a sec', Chloe. Must go behind a tree while there's still one left."

She did not seem to quite cotton on.

"Why?"

"You silly old idiot! Why d'you think?"

"Oh . . . you won't go far? You aren't just going to walk away from me, are you? You won't not come back?"

"You're still a silly old idiot," I assured her.

From where I eventually stood I found that I could still just see her down across the bracken. She waited there, in the middle of the track, quite a little way below me—standing in that inconsequential way people do when they just wait—holding our basket, shifting her weight idly from one foot to the other.

It was somehow marvelous that she should be waiting there for me.

Back in the sun we began to quicken our step. A certain air of excitement was beginning to come over Chloe.

"Steam engines used to make an awful fuss coming round this bit," she told me.

I was careful not to make any fuss. Far below now I could see the steep-sided valley between the mounds and then, as we completely rounded our side, I could see that our track led straight over it across a viaduct. There were five curving stone arches with a river wriggling down through the lofty center arch.

"Getting down's easier on the other side," Chloe said.

I could see that getting down was going to be quite a business. So was getting across. The single-track viaduct had no real walls or parapets. It went like a ruler for over five hundred yards before it got to the other side. They hadn't bothered to remove the old railway lines off the viaduct either.

"C'mon!" Chloe called over her shoulder.

She began running over the railway ties ahead of me. I followed, more gingerly, carrying the picnic basket, walking down the middle of the old rusting track, the sun full on me, walking from tie to tie. By the time she had got to the middle of the viaduct Chloe must have realized that I was not with her, for she stopped and waited.

I was walking farther and farther away from the real ground, my feet going from one old slat tie to the next, and somehow I felt I had no sides . . . I could only . . . sense somehow . . . the treetops in the valley underneath. I would not take the two-and-a-half steps to either side that would catapult me over; yet there was a hot and uncomfortable sense on the back of my neck that there was absolutely nothing to prevent me doing it.

I went on walking.

"Look, Matt," she called. She was pointing. "There it is."

But I was not looking to where she was pointing. All I could see was that she was stepping forward, that she was standing outside the rails, outside the ties and on the very edge.

Chloe's toes clutched round the edge of the viaduct brickwork.

I stopped still.

"Chloe—be careful," I said. I tried to say it softly, terrified that simply by speaking to her . . .

"I don't have to be careful."

I stared at her. She was so unconcerned. Yet there was nothing, nothing but the balance of her own body, between her and the reeling space down to the green valley floor. I had to put the picnic basket down. Just to manage to look—it was a peep only and to do that I had to kneel on the rusting track, and even then I felt cold and gooey.

"But I—*I* have to be careful," I said. "I'm sorry."

And then all at once she had realized and she had stepped back and was crouching on her heels beside me.

"Oh, Matt—I forgot—it's me that ought to be sorry. It's just what I shouldn't do. Look—can you bear to see?"

Chloe had to point before I could look, her face beside mine, her hair nearly in my eye, and only then did I realize what she wanted me to see.

I saw the river flowing through the water meadow far below, flowing between willows, bending leftward and widening to a sort of basin. It was like a small lake. On the far side there was a wall with a gap and a footbridge across it. Below the bridge there was an edge. It was only when I saw that edge that I heard the sound of distant roaring and knew what I was looking at.

It was the sound of many tons of pouring water.

"The weir," I croaked.

"Doesn't look very much, does it? Doesn't look anything. It's the way I went. I went alone. That's why I want you to come down with me. That's why I want to show it to you. I want to share it a little. It's become all mine, my property. . . . And I don't want it. I want to be rid of it."

She was holding on to me, I could feel her shaking, but I could only hold on to the rail, cling on to it and not say anything, frozen in the sun by where I was and what was happening.

"I'm so alone, Matt—so alone for so long. I'm trapped between where I was and where I'm going. But I am different from you. I have seen where I am going."

Her head looked away from me as she spoke but I knew that she was watching me from the corners of her eyes.

"D'you know, Matt—just now—had to stop myself. Be so easy—too easy—just to pull you a little, just to—for both of us to go over. So like to take you—to where I am. You could be there with me. You only have to let me let it happen."

Her tongue slid out between her teeth as if to taste . . . to taste this place she knew and that I did not know.

"It would be early for you, Matt. You see, until

124

you have really lived in your world, the next is no good. I know that it's only by living here that you can understand it there. I went too soon—far too soon! That's what happened to me. But some people are ready for us early. Perhaps if I showed you. . . . Perhaps it would be all right for you."

She looked full round at me.

"You've already had things, done things you wanted to do. People already know you can do things. You've begun. I've still to come to understand . . . and only when I do—and I don't know when or how— only when I understand and can forgive Mum and Dock and myself, only then shall I be able to begin in my turn, shall I be able to stop returning and returning."

I took a deep cold breath. I could see from her face that she meant so exactly what she said. And I felt afraid . . . so afraid for the Chloe I had come to know . . . and yet, most terrible of all, I felt, as I looked down over that sunny green void with its bright river, an enormous growing curiosity.

"Chloe," I said. It might have been an exclamation, it might have been a question, I might have been going to tell her—tell her what? Perhaps she was stronger than I. It wouldn't even be my fault. She had all the advantages. She could grab hold of me—and I could begin to feel myself wanting her to do it. She had only to push.

Yet suddenly she had let go of me, she was staring at me, had jumped back from me so that now she was sitting on her heels in the middle of the railroad ties, her hands gripping the rails, as if she, too, had become afraid of the viaduct.

"C'mon! Let's get to the other end, Matt. D'you hear it? Down below us? That's the Elverley River going over. When I hear it, it echoes in me! Over and over again . . . it's always going. It still hurts—changing worlds—and I have to keep changing so often, so often. But they both call, they both hurt, wherever I am. I must go down."

Chloe stood up. I found it difficult getting on my feet. I was shuddering, too. I couldn't take her hand. I couldn't take the basket. Chloe did seem to understand this for she took the basket from me and didn't laugh. She just walked on ahead. I knew I couldn't walk the other way. I knew I could not leave her. It would have been too cruel to have left her then. I did not want to leave Chloe. Yet if I were honest with myself I also knew that I was not really choosing. I tottered after her, over the wooden slats, looking neither left nor right, telling myself over and over again not to, telling my feet only to walk.

Almost at the end—and I was praying to get to that end, to get off this viaduct—Chloe maddened me by stopping.

"See the foam where the water slops over? D'you see where it goes mostly through the center?"

I didn't. I didn't want to. Yet even then I did not want Chloe to see me not wanting to see.

Chloe skipped on ahead. I just walked to the end of the viaduct, just walked on to its end. Just to put my foot down on soft soil again was like lifting a black curtain. I stood still.

She was waiting for me. She stood there, wrinkling up her freckled nose. The green eyes looked at me; they were concerned, I suppose they told me I was important.

"Thank you for coming, Matt," she said all over again.

"Thank you for asking me."

We sounded absurdly formal. Yet it was not absurd. I took hold of her hand. It was hot. Or mine was cold. We smiled. We giggled at each other like a pair of fools. We wrestled, we grabbed ahold of each other rather carefully and rolled over on the grass. We both knew we were not wrestling to fight but because it was a kind of conversation. When we stopped we sat apart from each other as if to think over what we had said.

11

We had left the disused railway. The roaring of the water was not so far away now. As we picked our way down the valley side it became more insistent—not enough to make it in any way difficult to talk, yet all the time it told me that we were coming to this one particular place.

The going down was almost easy. I went first and it was a zigzag path down through the bracken, and the roots of the trees were like steps. I caught glimpses of dragonflies. Spiderwebs touched at my mouth, my face. At times we were almost waist-deep in the bracken and here and there it was slippery underfoot. Once I had to grab at a tree trunk. Farther down I had to grab at Chloe as she slithered by me. We concentrated so hard on our feet that it was quite a shock to look up and discover that the viaduct arches were now curving high above our heads. We had to jump a small stream at the bottom and pick up the path again where it ducked beneath the green trailers of a weeping willow. All at once we had come out beside the Elverley River and its rock and grassy slopes and overhanging trees. It widened quite a way across.

"This is where we should have picnicked," I said.

"Didn't want to talk about this place *at* this place, Matt. And everything was different then—before the picnic."

We had stopped at the edge of the riverbank. I wondered what she was going to do. The water seemed so dark here under the willows and it moved so swiftly. It was smooth and if you did not look carefully you might almost have thought that it was still. But then all at once you would see a leaf, a twig, a feather go sweeping by.

Only we stood still.

I could see that the river led up to a long straight line, to a low stone wall. In the center of the stone wall was the gap, a gap with its narrow footbridge over, a bridge hardly wider than a gangplank and with a single rail. Under the bridge was an edge of water. It was from the edge of water that the river roared.

Chloe watched me.

"This is the place," she said flatly.

"The weir?"

"The weir is the way I have to go."

She must have read my face because she went on.

"Sometimes I stay here for days, sometimes a day or only half a day. Then I have to go. Have to go the way I went the first time. It calls me. I have to. It never quite stops calling whatever I do here. Sometimes it is only a distant murmur, other times it asks me, many times I am told, and I have to come here, whatever I am doing."

"Do you mean—do you have to go—over the weir?"

Chloe nodded.

"What is so stupid is that I am more frightened now than on that first day, although now I have done it often and often. D'you know I've never told Dock I have to come here. I could never have told my mum. Yet the story goes round in the village that I come. S'pose I've been seen, one time and another. I've tried not to be seen. But it's lonely by oneself—going over. Never ever anyone to say good-bye to me when I'm called, never anyone who could have said good-bye to me—before. I've so often had to go. So I thought, if ever I did have the courage to tell you who or what I was—that you might just come and see. Can you bear to?"

I could not help but look at the gap in the wall where the water roared tipped endlessly, relentlessly down to the level below. It took time for her words to make meanings in my head.

"After you met me—off the coach—you had to come here?"

"No. I haven't been here since you came here. But I know I must go on in a little while."

"Are—are you going now?"

"In a little while. When I am ready."

"Do I—won't I see you again? You're—you're not going forever now, are you?" All at once it gripped me, what she was doing.

130

"Dead people shouldn't come back. I'm not supposed to come back. But I'm tied to coming back. Might come back tomorrow. May have to come back. Want to see you again—oh, over and over again. Yet I want to go on, Matt. I so long to go on. Say you'll say good-bye to me today."

I am not sure that, at the time, I fully understood. I only understood that she was unhappy.

"Of course I will say good-bye. But I would rather say hello. And if you do come back tomorrow . . ."

Chloe turned away from the river as if to look back down the way we had come. There were the tall arches of the viaduct like high narrow windows on the valley up behind.

"Always had to come back. Always will 'til I believe I can go on. Only half a being over there. Can't let go—of this place. I take too much with me. Or I take the wrong things. No one tells me what the right things are. There was always my mum to tell me before, even if I didn't always agree with her. She could always make things work. She could always show me how to make things work. But she couldn't show me how to die. How could she have guessed that I would have been such a fool? And she was always so patient with me. I could always ask her again and again and she would always show me. Dad used to get cross if I got cold or stiff sitting for him. And now I can't be patient with my mum or help her back—even though she needs me. I can't begin to talk to her."

I put my hand on her arm. Yet I saw myself walking the long way back along the disused railway to Dockhurst's barn, alone. But I saw Chloe too, walking there, time after time. . . . And time after time coming back here after leaving her father, her mother.

And nobody really understanding why she was there at all. I did not understand. Yet I knew that I had become used to her, here and today. I simply liked her being here—and now that she was going to go away, she was not going to be here. I wanted her to walk all the way back with me. I wanted her to be not in any particular hurry, just talking of this and that. I wanted to go to sleep knowing that I would talk to her tomorrow.

Even then I kept forgetting what she was.

She was watching me.

"This is where I swam on that afternoon. Always have to swim from here now. This place."

"Chloe—what will you want me to do . . . . to say good-bye?"

For a moment she did not answer. She even turned aside and began to hunt around in the picnic basket. She dug about in there for what seemed an awfully long time. I could not see what she was looking for—at? Then at last she actually fished up a comb of her own and sat back on her heels to do her hair.

"Do, Matt? Just—just stand here and watch me swim out there, until you can't see me anymore. Wave to me, even if I can't see you waving. And be sorry that I'm going and be glad that I was here. Could you, Matt? Wish I could take you with me. . . . Or that I could really stay. But you must not come and I cannot stay."

I nodded. She could see from my face that of course I would wish her good-bye, if that was what she wanted me to do. But inside I didn't think saying good-bye was anywhere near enough.

She combed out her red hair so carefully. There

was still a streak of dirt on her face from the waiting room and, on an impulse, I wet my hand in the river and came back and wiped it off. Chloe smiled, put out her tongue at me, went on combing.

"Chloe, when you come back to us, do you arrive here?"

"No. Always arrive at the cottage where Mum lives, where we all used to live, by the rectory. My room's still there. It's not changed much. It's my room—where I always come back. That's where I open my eyes. My clothes have all gone now. Used to have a blue teddy bear called Glubb. Mum's chucked him. Think my wellingtons were the last to go. Mum didn't notice them on top of the wardrobe. But it's still my room. Of course, there's always the room at Dock's. But to me, Mum's is where I always come back. Yet I come here—when it's time to go on."

"Aren't you—aren't you tired of all these journeys?"

"Not tired, Matt. I can't be tired. Being tired doesn't happen now. But frightened—I'm always frightened of coming. What if Mum and Dock aren't here anymore? There wouldn't be anywhere to go on from. Yet this also frightens me—going on over the weir. You see, I'm not even sure who *is* going on. And that's worse than all the bumping. Nothing ever seems to be for the better. Today's the best day I've ever had, Matt. Just talking to you."

She plunged the comb back into the basket.

I looked down at her kneeling back on her heels in the grass, her T-shirt all grubby, her cotton skirt marked and creased from the walk, from Little Oaken station, from coming down the bank. I certainly knew

133

who she was. I had met her, eaten with her, gotten things for her, waited for her.

"Chloe, if you can't talk to your mum, why don't you tell Dock? You talk to him all the time. Tell him you don't know who you are."

An agonized look came over her face as she looked at me.

"I *can't! He's* got to find out. It's got to come from him. It's no good if it doesn't come from him. Yet I don't know what to do, Matt. He doesn't even try to find out now. P'raps—p'raps he's frightened of me. But I can't say. All I do is just go on and on like this and find out less and less. Everything's all slipping away. But what else can I do except come back?"

"You could do something for me, Chloe. Would you?"

She gaped at me.

"Tell me what I can do, Matt."

"Two things," I said. "First one will be easy for you. Do me—do me a couple of cartwheels."

Unexpectedly, she laughed.

"That's two things right there, Matt."

"One thing," I insisted. "You can. I've seen how you can. Do me two cartwheels."

She saw that I really meant it. For a moment she stood there, motionless, trying to decide why I should want her to. She seemed amused, flattered, puzzled . . . even a little shy. Then all at once she made up her mind, walked away, turned her back toward me— and turned them.

She turned them, first the one way and then the other. She could do them with a wonderful kind of lazy elegance, her feet pointing across the sky, one leg seeming so slow to follow the other, her hair sweeping the grass and then, perfectly, she was standing upright once again. And then she leaned the other way and it was as if the world turned and she hung still. Twice she made herself both inside out and upside down.

"Am I any good?" Chloe wanted to know.

"You're a lot of good," I told her.

"Well, if that's only one thing—what's the other?"

"You may not like me asking," I said cautiously.

"I'll do it if I can. Is it going to be difficult?"

"It won't be difficult. Not for you. But it may be the last thing you will do. I know you won't do it for Dock."

"Won't do it for Dock? What won't I ever do for Dock?"

"Not that I could ever do his bit of it as well as he can. And I haven't brought any of my stuff with me anyway. But I still want to ask you."

"Oh, Matt, you are making a lot of mysteries."

"Can't you remember, Chloe, that I really came down here to see your dad? He was going to teach me a bit. He'd promised to give me a whole week of drawing lessons. So this is the second thing I'm asking. I only want you to sit down—just there."

She did not quite know how to take me. She opened her mouth to protest—or to laugh, or to be pleased—and then shut it again. I shall never know which it was. Chloe sat.

I sat, too.

"I'm going to look at you," I said. "I haven't got a pencil and I haven't got a sketchbook. But Dock's been asking me to move an imaginary pencil in my head. So that's what I'm doing. And it's you that's sitting. I know you got fed up sitting for your dad, but this time you're sitting for me. That's what I'm asking you to do. And for you it won't make any difference that I am not putting pencil on paper. Sitting will be the same. And what I do for me isn't so important as what you are doing for you—sitting!"

"Don't mind sitting for you. Wish you really were drawing me."

"But I really am looking at you. Go on—turn your head a little more that way. . . . I can see your left ear coming out through your hair. And the way your nose tips up at the end. Now the smile's coming round. No—I'm being serious, please don't giggle—well, all right, you laugh, it changes the shape of your chin."

But she was also a shape against a willow tree and the bracken. Light against the bark of the tree, the light of her hair, the pale of her face. That's how I could have made the pale show up. At least I was being able to look at her as if I had been drawing—and looking is always what the drawing is all about. And Chloe was not any girl. She did take me perfectly seriously. I remember those lines coming up between her eyebrows.

"You're sitting back with your palms flat down on the grass and your feet stretched out in front of you. I can see the dirt lines on the soles of your feet. No—don't pull your feet up. You can wriggle your toes, if you like."

"Now you're not being serious," she complained, very seriously. "Perhaps I should move more if you're planning a drawing. Give you all the choices. If I do bring my knees up then how I sit all changes, doesn't it?"

I nodded.

"You know as much about it as I do, don't you, Chloe? You've sat for Dock so often. . . . You must have picked up all sorts of things from him. . . . Learned how to be a real model. You never sit awkwardly or too tight, do you?"

"Dad was fond of saying 'Chloe's never sat too tidy.' Mum was different. Always had to look scrubbed and tidy for Mum. But she could teach you how to dance. She said I was easy to teach, and maybe I was. But Mum could make the most hopeless people do it. Sure, I never could. She was always so patient with them."

". . . And knees are difficult. There's not much to go on with a knee, but if you get it wrong, it all goes wrong. But then, Chloe—you are good at swimming, too, aren't you? I mean, you *could* swim across the weir, in the ordinary way. However stupid it was, you did do it, when others couldn't."

"Trouble was, Matt—I thought it was important and nobody else did, or were too busy. And now I know that it wasn't a bit important, that it was stupid."

She was standing up on the tips of her toes and then slowly crouching down so that I could watch her kneecaps move. She even turned round so that I could see the backs of her knees too. Backs of knees aren't easy, either.

Chloe looked round at me over her shoulder.

"Me?" she asked shyly.

"You," I told her.

"Am I why—am I why you wanted me to do cartwheels?"

I ran a forefinger between the tendons on the back of her knee. She let me.

"That's how—that's how you told me who you were. Can't you feel it—even now, can't you feel it?"

The water roared on over the weir beyond her.

I remember her sitting on her heels in front of me, her green eyes searching my face from less than a foot away, and yet not saying anything to me, not saying a word.

I stared back.

All at once she jumped up and did me a whole row of cartwheels across the grass.

I can see her now, almost excited, standing on the edge of the bank with her back to the Elverley River. And then she had to walk up and down. When she stopped, she stood first on one leg and then on the other.

"Have to swim, Matt. Being called. I've—I've got to go on. You will say good-bye still? Want to come back tomorrow to see you again. Want to look at your sketchbook—if you'll let me. But I'm being called first. Being called awfully strong. P'raps nothing's different—but I have to go on to find out. I can't—can't stay here."

I could understand that she could not stay and yet I felt myself stepping out into some cold, sensible, unbearable misery. It was as if I had just reached across to her—and she was being snatched away. I did not want . . .

"Chloe—shall I wave to you from the bridge? I could wave to you so much longer from there."

"Oh please, Matt. But you must be quick. I—I
shall have to plunge in, in a minute. Please run, Matt,
for me. I shan't be able to stop myself."

She sat down. She stood up. She licked her lips
and kept tossing back her hair. I wanted to go up and
kiss her, hold her hand, put arms round her. . . . But
there was no time anymore.

"See you tomorrow, Chloe."

She hugged herself. She marked time with her
feet. She bent forward almost as if she were in pain.

"Hope tomorrow, Matt."

I ran.

I carried the picnic basket as I ran. I knew that
I could not have kissed her or said a proper good-bye
or anything. I only asked myself if I had helped her
or just made matters worse. I supposed that it wasn't
really my business. But what else could I have done?
I ran like mad.

Standing there on the slippery narrow catwalk,
the roar of the water was overwhelming. If it had not
been for Chloe I don't think I could have stood there.
The bridge was hardly three feet above the lip of the
weir but from over the lip one could see the water
foaming and falling to nearly fifteen feet below. I had
only one green rail to hang on to. The catwalk was
made of wooden slats and I could see the water swirl
beneath. Everywhere there was a spray so that my
face, legs, clothes—everything was soaked.

I waved.

Chloe looked so far away. She was still back there
on the bank, sitting crouched now, her hands locked
round her knees as if to keep herself still. She jumped
up when she saw my wave. All at once she was

released. She did not have to resist anymore. One hand waved back. . . . She made a powerful racing dive into the Elverley River, fully clothed.

For an instant I wondered why she had not stripped off and then, with a cold pang, remembered that all this was happening because she had insisted on swimming across the river fully dressed.

I watched. She swam a distinctly stylish crawl. Surely she could get across. She hadn't any shoes on. She wasn't wearing all that much. Yet something in Chloe herself steered her inexorably toward me, toward this roaring edge of the weir. It was very frightening. I saw her red hair spread out over the water behind her. I did not know if she could see me. But I waved, I waved madly.

And then it all happened because I glanced behind. I saw the water crashing down below. Chloe would never hear my shout. I also saw the top of the weir wall, just below me, just below the surface.

Chloe was coming. She had stopped swimming. Her face looked up at me, a hand was waving back, but it was a despairing face, she was coming with a terrible swoop under my feet.

I dropped flat, face down.

I simply could not stop myself. The roaring was in my ears. Chloe was going to go over, and I could not bear it.

Holding on with one hand I clutched down with the other—and I grabbed at Chloe's hair. I got it and did not let go. She was swept hard against the wall by the force of the water but I had stopped her going over. My feet managed to get a grip on the slats of the catwalk. Somehow I managed to get a hand under her

140

arm. I think she was screaming, I thought that for one awful endless instant I was going over with her, that we were both going to pitch down over the edge in each other's arms. I remember hanging upside down over space and spray and plummeting falling river. I shall never know how I got her back up onto the bridge. She fought me, then helped me, then I must have fainted.

I remember opening my eyes on a calm blue sky. I was lying in bracken and someone was bending over me. I could hear the sound of the weir but it now seemed very far away.

I was being asked, over and over again, if I was going to be all right.

I did not take too much notice at first. It did not seem to be of much importance. I tried, in a vague sort of way, to piece together everything that had happened. It was almost as if I were myself standing apart and watching myself come to. It even came as a sort of revelation to me that this person bending over me should be Chloe.

"Do, do say something, Matt," she was pleading.

Her hair hung in rattails and dripped down on me. Her T-shirt and briefs clung wetly to her. I had some sort of memory that she had lost her skirt getting back up onto the catwalk. I only knew now that she should not have come back. That it was all due to my sudden, stupid idiocy that she was *here*. And over and over again she was asking *me* if I was all right!

I had stopped her going on.

I blurted out that I was sorry. I realized that she must hate me. I should not have done it but I had not been able to help it. I said that I just hadn't been brave enough simply to stand there and let her slide over, to let her go. I told her that I had not wanted her to go.

She knelt down beside me as if to hear what I was trying to say. I just lay there listening to myself babbling my own nonsense. I can remember staring up at the droplets of water standing out on the freckles of her face, even on her eyelids, on the bridge of her nose. The water went on dripping down on me from the ends of her hair. I was realizing that she must equally have rescued me. But what so amazed me was how pleased she was to hear me speak.

"Shan't—couldn't ever hate you, Matt. You only wanted to save me. Taught me that I've always wanted to be saved—even though I've long been otherwise. That's something I've never realized properly until now. You see, on that silly afternoon when I first went over, when it all happened, I knew perfectly well that Dock and Mum couldn't possibly be there. Yet somehow I had always expected them to rescue me at the last moment. I've always resented the fact that they weren't there! Yet how could they have been? But for so long now I've still gone on feeling that they should have been there. Until this time. This time, you were there."

Her voice sounded perfectly clear and yet I can remember being convinced that it came from a very long way away. Yet I could feel the bracken under me, the sun's warmth, my own clothes clinging to me. I sat up a little. It seemed that I had not quite done the wrong thing.

"—Long as you're all right, Matt. You tried so

hard for me. Sorry if I winded you. You have the knack of doing all the right things."

I told her that now I had no idea what to do.

"Poor Matt. You've got the hardest thing of all yet."

I saw that she was excited—concerned, too—but bubbling over underneath.

"Don't you understand, Matt—I shan't have to come back, not anymore. Shan't have to go on by going over the weir—I'm freed of all that, thanks to you. This is the end of being half here. I can change. I've become free, but the first thing I have to do is to hurt you—have to ask you to put up with me hurting you by going away. Because I'm free—I can't choose anymore—I have to go."

But I did not understand then. I had to tell her that she was sopping wet, that we had to get her dry and home. I only made her laugh.

"Don't you see it doesn't matter—not where I'm going. I have to go where it is always otherwise and always home. Funny, isn't it—you've helped me to go on because you wanted me to stay. You keep forgetting what I am, don't you? Perhaps I forget it, too. But it means being more real. Waited so long to be properly real. Waited so long to let go."

Even then, her words did not fully penetrate. Looking back, possibly she had already begun to go, though I had not realized. I asked her what I should tell her mother—and Dock. I did not know what to tell myself.

"They'll know. Say—say thank you for me. Not any special message. Mustn't be any special message. I've talked too much anyway."

I think it was a little later, when I was watching her squeezing the water out of her hair, twisting it like a red rope, her back turned to me, her head down, it was then that I knew that she was going forever. I opened my mouth and shut my mouth and could only say nothing.

"You didn't half pull," she was telling me. "Thought my head would come off when you grabbed for me."

I managed to smile a little.

And then I knew there was a question I had to ask while I still could.

"Chloe, your mother told me something about the Elverley dance. She said it was a dance of death. Was that the secret?"

She pushed her hair back over her shoulders and shook her head.

"No, Matt. The dance of Elverley is the dance of life. The other dancers—to the Brat, they are ghosts . . . like you. They dance every year before the Brat comes. And when it has gone—they still dance dully on. The Brat is the individual spark. The Brat dances out of life into this world and out of this world back into life again."

"You are the Brat really—aren't you, Chloe?"

"Sometimes. But for me . . . for me, the Brat happens to be you."

I sat full up at that. I could see that Chloe was right. But already she had turned away.

"Don't forget the picnic basket," she reminded me. "Dock's always using it on his expeditions. Hangs up behind the kitchen door."

I told her I would not forget. I did not say to her that I did not want her to go—that I could not bear her to go. I did not say that I was sitting there wishing that I had not helped at all. I knew that it was a stupid wish—and went on wishing it.

"Matt?" she was asking.

"Mmmmmm."

"Will you promise not to make fun of me if I take these wet things off? You won't laugh?"

I did not quite know why but I found myself more alarmed than laughing.

"I expect you're getting cold, aren't you?" I tried to sound full of common sense.

"Not that. It's that I can't take anything with me now. Mustn't take any of your world with me. Mustn't take anything with me 'cept myself."

It was then that I knew that she was going farther away than I could ever imagine.

"I shan't laugh at you. But are you sure you want me to be here?"

"Please stay, Matt. If you don't mind. Just to be here and to say good-bye, to see me go and know that I've gone."

She turned away, tugged off her things and dropped them in the grass. She was a little awkward over it, perhaps because they were so wet. Even without them she still looked a bit goosey, a bit like a drowned rat. She came back and stood in the sun, the mass of freckles about her shoulders and midriff, her dark red hair; yet, although she stood close to me, she seemed already to be farther away.

"I—I wanted to draw you like that, Chloe. But I would never have had the courage to ask."

Chloe nodded, she appeared to half hear, she appeared to listen and to understand.

It was then that I knew that she was about to go.

I struggled up onto my feet. I was still shaky. My ears were still full of the roar of the weir. Looking at it, the surface of the river still seemed so motionless. The green mounds of Elverley stood high above us, the forgotten railway hung over our heads. I would have to find my own way back.

"How—how are you going on?" I ventured to ask.

"I'll just go. No—don't come any nearer to me. You mustn't touch me now. I want to wish you so well. Want you to remember me. Want you to remember an ordinary girl you just happened to meet. That's what I am. As others are—so I was. As I am—so will they be. You must not be sorry for me for being what I am. Only sorry that we shan't see each other again. It is good where I go. And good not to come back. Good for everyone. Say good-bye for me. Say good-bye to me and watch me go. I shall go far away but I shall remember. No, stay where you are. Only . . . only say good-bye."

I think I can remember hearing my own voice saying that good-bye. But what I remember more clearly is Chloe herself, standing there in the green bracken, her feet a little apart, her hands on her hips, looking away from me . . . and waiting. Yet I am certain that it was I who sent her away. It was as if my attention faltered, as if my watching attention had become unable to hold her together. Her freckles became dots of brown, she became a splurge of red lost in the green and the gray of the river, in the touches of blue. She, her hair, her face, her shape, became streak and line and spot. What I had known as Chloe did not go away but became otherwise. Chloe had become marks made across my mind. What had once made Chloe raised a hand within my head and waved.

Mr. and Mrs. Dockhurst came over the grass, toward me, together. Their relief at finding me was obvious. The way they came toward me—I might almost have been Chloe. I must have looked very shocked and stunned.

"She—she won't come back again. She'll never come back now."

For a long time I did not say anything more.

They had brought some things with them. They were very kind. They made me drink something. I can hardly remember what they said. I have an odd memory of part of me being quite happy and yet the tears came streaming down my face. Not that it mattered with them. It did seem an endless way back and we all went to their first cottage, the one by the rectory. That night we all stayed there. Hester sang us the old songs, about the Brat and the barley harvest and the one gate that must be opened that every villager may at last go dancing through. Dockhurst and Hester laughed together and Dockhurst drew her, singing. I slept in Chloe's old room.